Yr 5 Rm 10

*Gettin*

GREENGATE COUNTY JUNIOR SCHOOL

*For Frances Foster,*
*who's been teaching me how to write*

# Getting Even

*Mavis Jukes*

Teens · Mandarin

First published in Great Britain 1989
by William Heinemann Ltd
Published 1991 by Teens Mandarin
an imprint of Mandarin Paperbacks
Michelin House, 81 Fulham Road, London SW3 6RB

Mandarin is an imprint of the Octopus Publishing Group

Copyright © 1988 by Mavis Jukes

This edition published by arrangement with
Alfred A. Knopf, Inc., USA

ISBN 0 7497 0330 X

A CIP catalogue record for this title
is available from the British Library

Printed in Great Britain
by Cox and Wyman Ltd, Reading, Berkshire

# 1

MAGGIE SAT UP and moved the curtain away from the window. She could see her father standing under the porch light, talking and laughing softly with Samantha. Samantha was barefoot; she was holding her high-heeled shoes by the straps.

Maggie watched as her father leaned down and kissed Samantha, watched as he held her against him for a moment, with his cheek resting on her hair.

Maggie let the curtain fall and looked at the clock; the red numbers were glowing. It was two twenty-three in the morning.

She heard Samantha's car start up and rumble out of the driveway and away down the road. She heard her father shut the front door and come up the stairs, heard him loudly brush his teeth and spit the toothpaste into the sink. A moment later the line of light under her bedroom door went black.

In the bottom bunk her sister was asleep and gently snoring. Maggie lay for a while in the darkness, thinking.

So Samantha was her father's girlfriend – that was pretty plain to see. Why didn't he just say so?

Maggie kicked at some books at the foot of her bed that were bothering her, then sat up and moved them against the wall. She felt around for her cloth rabbit. It was wedged between the mattress and the headboard; she pulled it out by the ears and held it against her body, under her chin.

The next thing she knew, it was morning.

It was morning, and Maggie could hear her father downstairs in the kitchen, clattering dishes. She rolled over and stared at the pattern of sunlight on the wall.

So, her father had a girlfriend.

Maggie sat up; she had an uneasy feeling in her stomach, as if she'd done something wrong.

But it wasn't wrong to wake up and look out of the window. And was there a law against a man kissing a woman good-bye in the middle of the night?

Maggie threw back her covers and climbed down the ladder. What was there to feel bad about? Her parents had been divorced for more than two years; her mother didn't even want to be married to her father any more.

She looked through the rungs at her little sister, Dinah, who was sleeping the wrong way round on the blankets with her feet on the pillow.

She tiptoed out of the room.

Her father was reading the newspaper at the kitchen table. "Tired, Dad?" Maggie asked him.

"No, why?"

Maggie said nothing.

He put down the newspaper and looked at her. "Hungry?"

She nodded.

He fixed her Rice Krispies with sliced banana. And her stomach began to feel better. See? Nothing was wrong. She was just hungry. There wasn't anything wrong with her father having a woman for a friend – especially if the woman was Samantha.

"How late did you stay up last night?" she said.

"I didn't look at the clock."

Maggie stared at him as she ate.

"Why are you looking at me like that?"

"Like what?" said Maggie. "There's crumbs in your moustache." She picked up her bowl and drank the rest of the milk out of it.

"Sick!" she cried. She frowned at a hair stuck to the bottom of the bowl. "Everything has hair in it!"

"Oh, come on, now. Don't exaggerate," said her father. He put his hand on his chest. "And *pardon* me. Next time, fix your own cereal."

"Listen," said Maggie, "Nobody's exaggerating. Every weekend when I'm here, Blossom sneaks up onto my bed at home and gets dog hair all over my pillow."

"Well, I can't be held responsible for what happens at your mother's house. But why don't you shut your bedroom door?"

Maggie didn't answer. "Plus," she continued, "on Friday, Corky Newton put hair in my sandwich."

Her father made a face. "Why did you let him do that?"

"Let him?" said Maggie. "*Let* him? Nobody let him, Dad. He did it when I wasn't looking."

"Then how do you know he was the one who did it?"

"Dad, some things you just know. He always does things like that to people. Of course, he's the principal's nephew, so naturally I can never get even with him. And he's a sneak! I can't catch him at anything! If I try, he just threatens to report me. He's the clean-up captain."

"Report you for what?"

"For anything. How do I know?"

"He's the clean-up captain, and he puts hair in people's lunches?"

"Yes."

Maggie's father picked up the newspaper and turned a page. "Well, I think that's highly inappropriate – it's an abuse of power."

Maggie said nothing.

"And," said her father from behind the newspaper, "I think he needs a taste of his own medicine."

Maggie said nothing.

Her father folded down one corner of the newspaper and looked at her. "You need to get even with him."

"Look, Dad," said Maggie. "The guy's a foot taller than I am. And he's an animal – he can kick a ball over the west yard fence!"

Her father kept looking at her. Then he smiled a crooked smile. "But you're a Hunter, and the Hunters don't take any baloney from anybody." He reached over and messed up Maggie's hair. "Look in the mirror! Look at that Hunter beak. Look at those eyeteeth! You're Daddy's girl, honey. You're a fox! A sly fox," he added in a whisper, "who can outsmart anybody – anybody! Including clean-up captains," he said, his eyes glimmering. "And principals' nephews!"

"Dad," said Maggie.

Her father put the newspaper on the table. "Dad, nothing. Let me tell you something," he said. "When I was a freshman at Harvard, a guy on the football team – a linebacker – kept sneaking into the bathroom and putting honey in my shoes every time I took them off to take a shower."

4

Maggie looked at him. "Well, why didn't you lock the bathroom door?"

Her father took a large swallow of juice. "No lock."

"How did you know he was the one who was doing it?"

"The same way you know Corky Newton trashed your lunch. Some things you just know. Anyway, I got tired of having sticky feet. So one time when he went away for the weekend, I borrowed a pig from my cousin in New Hampshire. And I locked it in his dorm room. Of course, a pig has to eat, so I dumped in a couple of trash cans full of rotten food that I found outside the cafeteria."

Maggie smiled.

Her father smiled back.

"Needless to say," he said, "the guy never messed with me again."

Maggie folded her hands behind her head and tipped back her chair. "Did you get into trouble?"

"Nope."

"Nobody told him it was you?"

"Are you kidding? Of course not! We never ratted on each other – ever. In fact, a bunch of guys in the hall chipped in and bought me a pizza when they found out about it." He winked at Maggie. "It was really great!"

"Dad?"

"What?"

"Let me ask you something. If you thought it was so funny to shut a pig in a guy's room when you were in college, then why did you get so mad when Iris shut Richard in your briefcase?"

Her father frowned. "That's an entirely different matter. And it was entirely unprovoked." He looked at Maggie and she bit her bottom lip to keep from smiling. "What's so funny about shutting a hamster in my briefcase? My secretary had to recopy my entire appointment book."

"Nothing."

"Right. Nothing is funny about Iris – she's a total pain."

Maggie stood up and put her bowl in the sink. "You know, you really sound just like Mum."

"Your mother also thinks Iris is a pain in the neck? Remarkable! We actually agree on something."

"Congratulations," said Maggie. "Both of you hate my best friend. But I have a little news for you," she said, turning to face her father. "Iris and I are going to have a band together, whether you hate her or not."

Her father closed his eyes and slowly shook his head. "A band with Iris," he muttered. "I can just imagine it."

"We are!" cried Maggie. "She has a keyboard, and she can make it sound like anything she wants, including an electric guitar. And an electric violin! Plus, her parents might buy her drum pads that you can plug into it." Maggie paused. "And *you cannot* 'just imagine it'! You don't understand music and art. All you understand are lawsuits. And tweed suits!"

"Now look who sounds just like your mother."

"Well, it's true. All you care about are Apple computers."

"Boy!" said her father, standing up and brushing some crumbs from his lap. "What a grump. Somebody must have got up on the wrong side of the bed this morning. Or stayed up too late last night."

"Stayed up too late last night? *Me?*" said Maggie. She chuckled a little. "You should talk."

6

"What's that suppose to mean?" said her father.

"Oh, nothing," said Maggie. "But speaking of staying up *late* last night. *Samantha* thinks the band is a great idea. I told her about it. She said she had a band when she was a kid."

"Yes, but not with somebody like Iris," said Maggie's father.

Maggie turned away from him.

"Oh come on," he said, putting his arm around her shoulder, "I'm only teasing you." But Maggie shrugged him away. "Have a band with Iris," he said. "And if you ever need a drummer to sit in with you, hey, I'm your man! Dave the Rave." He began drumming a rhythm on the wall by the door. "I used to be a champ at drumming!"

"Sure, Dad."

He drummed harder and nodded his head to the rhythm. "I did! Bongo drums! In my hippie phase, as your mother describes it."

"Right," said Maggie.

"You think I'm kidding? I'm telling you – when I was in law school, I used to go down to the park on Saturday afternoons and drum with some guys that hung out there."

"Sure."

"What do you mean, 'sure'? You think you and Iris invented the drums? I played the drums before you were born! Of course, your mother discouraged me. She laughed at me, so I quit. But once I drummed for eleven hours in a rally for peace in Vietnam. Eleven hours straight!" He grabbed the salad servers from the draining board and began rapping on a lid.

Maggie ignored him. "I'm going to wake up Dinah. Mum said she'd be picking us up early this weekend."

7

Maggie went upstairs. She resented the way her father talked about Iris. What was so bad about Iris, anyway?

Maggie took off her nightgown, stuffed it into her overnight case, and zipped the top.

So Iris's hamster had peed on his appointment book. So, big deal.

She unzipped the side pocket of the bag and found white cotton pants, a white cotton vest and a T-shirt with a gorilla skateboarding on the front. She balled up the vest and crammed it back in.

Dinah opened her eyes. "Get up," Maggie told her. She dived into the bottom bunk and began tickling Dinah's feet. "Get up, get dressed. Mum's going to be here soon, and she hates it when we're not ready."

Maggie helped Dinah put on her clothes, and they went downstairs. The front door was open, and their father was outside. Samantha's red convertible Porsche was parked near the garage.

"Sam!" shouted Maggie from the doorway.

Maggie and Dinah ran out to the car.

"Back again," said Samantha. "I raced over to Macy's at nine thirty this morning. There was something there that I *had* to get you." She reached into the back seat for a maroon paper bag.

"This is for you," she said to Dinah, handing her a chocolate bear wrapped in foil. Dinah tore it open.

Then Samantha sang out trumpet noises and pulled a pair of black lace fingerless gloves out of the bag. "And these are for you," she said to Maggie. "Every lead singer in a band needs a pair of these."

Carefully fitting her fingers through the holes, Maggie put on the gloves and stretched the lace up to

8

her elbows. She held out her arms and stared at them. "Thanks," she said to Samantha.

The gloves looked fantastic. And Iris would have a fit when she saw them! Iris – whose mother let her shop in vintage clothing stores like the big kids did, whose mother let her wear huge balloony shorts and high-top sneakers splashed with acrylic paint to school – didn't have a pair of black fingerless gloves. Yet.

Maggie's father walked over. Samantha moved her sunglasses from the bridge of her nose to the top of her head and looked up at him. He gazed into her eyes.

For some reason Maggie felt her face grow hot.

She looked away.

Dinah tugged on her father's trouser leg. "I've eaten a bear. And look at Maggie's gloves."

Her father turned round. "Pretty snazzy," he said to Maggie. "But do you think your mother will approve?" He pulled his shirt cuff away from his watch. "And speaking of your mother, what time did she say she was coming to pick you up?"

"Eleven o'clock," said Maggie. She took off the gloves and jammed them into her front pocket.

He showed Samantha the face of his watch, and Samantha said, "Well, I'd better hit the bricks!" and hopped into the convertible without even opening the door. She moved her sunglasses down onto her nose. "Good-bye, girls! See you next weekend maybe, huh?"

Samantha shifted into reverse. "Dig you later!" she called.

Maggie watched the car grow smaller as it headed down the road.

"Well," said Maggie's father. "All packed?"

Maggie nodded.

"How about you, Dinah?"

"Perkins is packing," said Dinah.

"Oh, right!" said Maggie.

Her father looked down at Dinah. "Perkins is packing?"

"Yup."

"How much has he packed?"

"Nothing."

Maggie glared at her father. "Why do you go along with that see-through runt? I hate Perkins!"

"Relax," said her father. "You had an imaginary friend once, too, you know."

"Yeah, well, I'm sick of Perkins," said Maggie. "You don't have to hear about Perkins all week long. You only have to hear about him on the weekends."

At that moment Maggie's mother drove up to the house in a beat-up Chevy.

"See?" said Maggie. "I knew Dinah wouldn't be ready."

Their mother got out of the car and walked up the path with one hand in the pocket of her overalls. "Hi, girls," she said. She gave Maggie a long squeeze. "I missed you."

Maggie squeezed her back. She felt a little guilty, because she hadn't missed her mother. But the weekend had gone by so fast! Samantha had been there all day Saturday; they'd taken a picnic to the park, flown kites, fed M&M's to the ducks. They'd had pizza for supper, then stayed up late watching *Pinocchio* on the video.

Her mother smoothed the top of Dinah's head. "Ready to go?"

Maggie ran into the house and up to the bedroom.

She crammed everything of Dinah's into Dinah's duffle bag, picked up her own overnight case, and hurried outside.

"Now, what about next weekend?" Maggie's father was saying to her mother. "Same as this weekend? I get Dinah at your place and pick up Maggie after school?"

Maggie's mother shrugged. "I'll give you a call." She walked down the path.

"Good-bye, Rose," said Maggie's father politely, but her mother didn't seem to hear him. She just kept on walking, and Maggie wished more than anything that her mother would turn and say good-bye.

He kissed Dinah and Maggie. "Remember," he whispered to Maggie, "the Hunters don't take any guff from anybody." And they did thumbs-up to each other before she headed to the car.

# 2

"So," said Maggie's mother as they drove away. "How was the weekend?"

"Good," said Maggie. "We went on a picnic."

"And I made lemon sandwiches," said Dinah.

Her mother moaned. "Not again!"

"Again," said Maggie.

"Why your father allows a four-year-old to make sandwiches that he knows nobody will eat is beyond me."

"Sam ate one," said Dinah.

Her mother glanced at her in the rearview mirror. "Rind and all? And seeds? Good for Sam. Who's Sam?"

"A lawyer who works in Dad's office," said Maggie. She quickly changed the subject. "Speaking of gross sandwiches, you won't believe what happened to me at school on Friday."

"What?"

"Corky Newton cleaned out Iris's hairbrush and put the ball of hair in my sandwich."

"You're not serious! Did you speak to Mrs Hall about it?"

"No," said Maggie. "Mrs Hall wasn't there. We had a supply teacher."

"Did you tell her?"

"Yes, but she said I didn't know for sure that Corky Newton did it."

"Well, do you know he did it?"

"Yes."

"How?"

"Iris and I figured it out."

"Really," said her mother. "That's interesting." She looked sideways at Maggie. "Are you sure it wasn't Iris who did it?"

"Mum!" said Maggie. "Why would Iris put hair in my sandwich?"

"Well, she gave Dinah chewing gum with fish food in it." She looked again at Maggie. "What's so funny? Do you know what fish food is? Dried bugs."

"But Dinah liked it."

"Yes. And she also likes lemon sandwiches, but that's not the point."

"Well, anyway," said Maggie. "Corky did it and I'll tell you how I know." She cleared her throat. "One, he sat on the lawn to eat so he could watch me eat, and he never sits on the lawn by the picnic tables. He always sits by himself on the bench, by the tetherball pole, which he considers his own personal property.

"Two," continued, Maggie, "he laughed when I took a bite."

"You took a bite?" said her mother. She stopped at the stop sign, closed her eyes for a moment, and shook her head. "That is really revolting!"

"Three," said Maggie, "Corky Newton is clean-up captain."

"And what does that have to do with it?"

"Well, he's the only one who has the opportunity to snoop around the lunches in the cloakroom during class time. And four, he's a total jerk."

"The clean-up captain has to snoop around the lunches? Why?"

"He's supposed to give a morning report on the neatness of the classroom to Mrs Hall. And if he discovers problems with litter outside the classroom, in the halls, or on the school grounds, he's supposed to report it directly to the principal's office. He wears a sheriff's badge to school!"

"My word! He must take his job seriously."

"Well, the principal gave them out. Little metal ones. One for every clean-up captain, one clean-up captain for every room. Corky Newton pins his on his back pocket. He's a total nerd. Iris calls him Badge Butt."

"Go on," said her mother.

"Okay," said Maggie. "So anyway, his job includes checking the cloakroom for litter, and that's where the coatrack is. We keep our lunches under the coatrack, and Iris keeps her hairbrush in her coat pocket."

"I'm beginning to get the picture," said Maggie's mother. She slowed the car to go over some railway tracks. "But still and all," she said, "it doesn't prove that Corky Newton did it."

"Oh, ha!" said Maggie. "Who else had the opportunity to be around my lunch and a hairbrush without anybody looking? Unless –" Maggie looked thoughtful. She turned and stared at Dinah. "Did you put a wad of hair in my sandwich before I left for school last Friday?"

"No," said Dinah.

"Did Perkins?"

"No," said Dinah.

Maggie turned round. "It was Corky Newton," she told her mother.

"Well, you must definitely speak to Mrs Hall about this tomorrow."

Maggie rolled down the window and put her elbow out. She saw a girl squirt a boy with a garden hose and race away. "Oh, I don't know about that."

"What do you mean, you 'don't know about that'?"

"Dad said I should give Corky Newton a taste of his own medicine."

"Oh, he did, did he?"

"Yup." Maggie looked at herself in the mirror and checked out her profile with the wind blowing her hair back. "He said the Hunters never take any baloney from anybody. When he was in Harvard, he put a pig in a guy's room once – to get even with him. And everybody bought him a pizza."

"Harvard," muttered Maggie's mother. She stopped at a blinking red light. She slowly looked both ways and then drove through the intersection, shifting from one gear to the next without speaking. "You need to talk to Mrs Hall," she said. "Tomorrow."

"Why?" said Maggie.

"Because you're not at Harvard, that's why. You're at Franklin Middle School."

Maggie's mother glanced at her. "Look," her mother said in a serious voice. "Let me explain something to you. When your father was a kid, he went to some prep school in Vermont for rich kids. They wore knee socks and shorts. They wore blazers! Then he went to Harvard. Now, how would he know how to solve the kinds of problems kids have in the real world? How?"

Maggie didn't answer.

"Maggie, I've been listening to those Harvard stories for years. And let me tell you something: you're

15

in a completely different situation. Your father shouldn't advise you to get even with Corky Newton. This isn't a game! You'll get a black eye or a bloody nose – or you'll end up getting tossed out of school. And in the end, who do you think is going to buy you a pizza?"

Maggie shrugged.

"Nobody," said her mother. "Your father's attitude may work for him, because he's a lawyer. But this 'getting even' stuff doesn't work for a fifth-grade girl. It's easy for him to say 'the Hunters don't take any baloney from anybody.' He just turns around and sues people who make him mad! In your case, retaliating will aggravate the problem, not solve it. You need to get help from the adults in charge at your school."

Maggie stared at her mother. "Getting even isn't just for lawyers. Dad wasn't a lawyer when he put the pig in the guy's room."

"Now you're telling me when your father became a lawyer? I know exactly when your father became a lawyer. I waited on him hand and foot for four months while he studied for the bar exam.

"And I know all about that pig incident, too – although I'd just as soon forget it. You think I don't know about that pig? Do you know how many times I chased that pig out of our garden?"

"No," said Maggie.

"You're right, you don't," said her mother.

"Let's play the animal game," said Dinah.

"How many times?" said Maggie.

"Many, *many* times," said her mother. "I was all too well acquainted with that particular hog. I lived next door to your father's cousin, on a farm in New Hampshire. He didn't mention that?"

"No," said Maggie.

Her mother cleared her throat. "Your father would come to the country to visit his cousin, wearing a tweed jacket and leather elbow patches and a necktie. He'd come up and yak to me over the fence about being on the squash team. Wearing a necktie. Can you imagine it? That's what the boys at Harvard do to entertain themselves when they're not locking pigs in other people's rooms. They play squash. Squash! And there I was, *raising* squash – digging in the earth while he courted me. You didn't know I worked on my father's farm?"

"No."

"Well, now you know. I dropped out of junior college to help my father on the farm."

"Okay," said Maggie.

"And I'll tell you something, sweet pea. This farm girl knows plenty of things about school your father doesn't know, degree or no degree. Does he have any idea that you are in a mixed age-group classroom and that this Newton kid is at least a year older than you are?"

She glanced at Maggie, and Maggie shrugged.

"Does he know that Corky Newton is the principal's nephew?"

"Yes."

"Great! Get back at the principal's nephew for something he may not even have done? Your father's a lawyer! Is that his idea of justice?"

Maggie said nothing.

"Let's play the animal game," said Dinah.

"Let's not," said Maggie.

"Play the animal game," said Maggie's mother. "Dinah's been sitting so quietly. Pay some attention to your sister."

Maggie sighed. She saw a horse standing in a field of stubble, swishing its tail. "Is it a horse?"

"No," said Dinah.

"I quit," said Maggie.

"No, you don't quit," said Maggie's mother. "Play the game." She drummed her fingers on the steering wheel.

"Well, first can I ask you something? Without your getting mad?"

"What?"

"Never mind."

"What!"

Maggie smiled a little. "It's about when Dad was in law school."

Her mother sighed. "What is it you want to know?"

"Did Dad really play the bongo drums in his hippie face?"

"Hippie *phase*," said her mother. They drove past a white farmhouse. A goat with whiskers was tied to the mailbox at the end of the driveway. "Although he did have a hippie face, come to think of it. He wore a beret and a goatee and played drums with some derelicts at the park, yes."

"Was it funny?"

"No. It was certainly *not* funny. He played drums in the park while I slung hash and worked as a waitress to make money to pay his tuition so he could end up making a hundred and fifty thousand dollars a year."

"I meant, was *he* funny? He said you laughed at him."

"That's what he said? That I laughed at him? Well that really takes the cake," said Maggie's mother. "I did *not* laugh at him. He's got it wrong way round, as usual. *He* laughed at *me* – at all my creative ventures,

18

including the ceramic art pieces I used to make with animals painted on them!"

"Okay," said Maggie.

"Play the animal game!" cried Dinah.

Maggie sighed and looked out of the window. "Is it a bird?" she said to Dinah.

A vulture was circling in the air.

# 3

THE NEXT AFTERNOON, after school, Maggie and Iris walked along the pavement towards Iris's house. The air was sweet and smoky; somebody was burning leaves. Ahead of them walked a woman carrying a baby in a backpack. The baby was bundled up; his hat had fallen down over his eyes.

"See all the pretty trees? See the pretty leaves?" the mother was saying to the baby. "See the birdie? The birdie is getting ready to fly bye-bye for the winter!"

Iris nudged Maggie and whispered. "Let's get past her. She's nuts!"

They passed on either side.

"So," said Iris. "Getting back to this Corky Newton thing – I think you've made a good decision."

Maggie said nothing.

"It was smart not to tell Mrs Hall that Badge Butt trashed your lunch last Friday. Your father has the right idea."

"You think?"

"Yes, I think," said Iris. "Corky Newton definitely needs a taste of his own medicine." She patted Maggie on the back. "So all you have to do is figure out how to get him back, right?"

"Well, I haven't completely made up my mind yet. I

20

just didn't tell Mrs Hall today. I might tell her tomorrow, like my mum wants me to."

A boy on a bike rode past, singing a song about somebody's girdle. He tossed a chocolate wrapper in the air.

"There goes Corky Newton now," said Iris. "What a pig."

The wind blew the wrapper under a parked car. "I can't believe Mrs Hall would let him be clean-up captain."

"Me either," said Maggie. "But what else do you expect? He's the principal's nephew, and you know what a clean-up freak the principal is."

"You can say that again," said Iris. "And you know what? Hilary told me that Corky Newton snooped in her desk and found peppermints and told Hilary that he's going to report her in his morning clean-up captain's report unless she gives him one sweet every day."

Maggie stopped and looked at Iris. "You're kidding."

"I'm serious. And you know what he does? He tosses the empty wrappers under the desk as a reminder. As a threat! She's a wreck about it! And she's running out of peppermints!"

"That's extortion!" said Maggie.

"Exactly what I told her," said Iris.

They started walking again.

"Well, he'd better not look in my desk," said Maggie. "I've got a sanitary pad in my desk, in case I start my period in school."

"Fat chance," said Iris.

Maggie said nothing. She just kept looking at her shoes and avoiding the cracks in the sidewalk. Hilary really ought to tell on Corky Newton, she decided. She was the one who should tell! Extortion was a serious offence – more serious than putting hair in somebody's sandwich.

"I hope Hilary tells on Corky Newton, that's what I hope," said Maggie. "That's what my mum says *I* ought to do."

"Yeah, well, you're not Hilary, so I think you'd better listen to your dad," said Iris. She looked sideways at Maggie. "Face it. Hilary's a wimp."

"But my mum says maybe Corky Newton didn't put hair in my sandwich – maybe he wasn't the one."

"He was the one," said Iris.

Maggie moved a strap of her backpack from one shoulder to the other. "Well, he did ask me if there was any sand in my sandwich today."

"See?" said Iris. They turned up the path to her house.

"And he picked up my ponytail and looked underneath," said Maggie. "And he turned around and made a pig noise at me during the spelling test."

Maggie and Iris trudged up the front steps to Iris's house. "Plus he calls me monkey arms. Why does he hate me?" said Maggie.

Iris opened the door. "I'm home!"

"Wipe your feet!" called the housekeeper from upstairs. "Is Maggie with you?"

"Yup!"

"Hello, Mrs Fuller!" called Maggie.

"Hello, Maggie!"

The vacuum cleaner started.

Maggie put her backpack by the hat stand next to the door.

"Well, if I do decide to get him back, what would I do?"

She and Iris walked into the kitchen. Maggie sat down and spun the salt shaker on the table.

Iris caught the salt shaker and dumped some salt on the table and drew a path through it with her finger. "Funny you should ask," she said. "Because I just happened to get an idea about that when we passed that baby on the way home." She pushed a box of chocolates towards Maggie. "Have one. Myself? I've given them up. "She opened up her mouth and looked at her teeth in the toaster. "And I have to go to the dentist tomorrow."

Maggie lifted the lid and searched through the brown pleated paper wrappers. "This box is empty."

Iris laughed a little to herself. Then she put the lid back on the box and threw it Frisbee-style into the bin. "Follow me," she said to Maggie. She got up and walked over and opened the refrigerator door. "Smell something?"

Maggie took a deep breath. She shook her head.

Iris took Maggie's sleeve, pulling her closer to the bottom shelf. "Now do you smell it?"

"Yes!" cried Maggie. "P.U.!"

Iris picked up a round box with French words printed on it in red and black ink. "It's Camembert cheese," she said, "from France. It's really ripe. More commonly known as stinkola cheese." She kissed the box. "Take a whiff!"

"Ick," said Maggie.

"You should smell it with the wrapper off!"

"No, thanks," said Maggie. "Put it back."

"It smells like a dirty nappy," said Iris.

"I believe it. Put it back."

Iris looked at Maggie and smiled a thin smile. "Wouldn't it be embarrassing if someone were to get this, say, on his clothes?"

"Yes!" said Maggie.

She quickly moved away from Iris.

"In particular," said Iris, "wouldn't it be awful if someone were to get this on the back of his pants . . . at school?"

They stared at each other for a minute.

"Are you thinking what I'm thinking?" said Maggie.

They both smiled.

Iris put the box of cheese on the cutting board and got out a knife.

"I'm not saying I'll do this," said Maggie.

"Fine," said Iris. She shook the lid off the box.

"It's bad to waste food!" said Maggie. "Look! It says five dollars and ninety-five cents!" She pointed to the sticker on the box.

"Give me a break," said Iris. "Did Badge Butt think about wasting food when he trashed your sandwich?"

"Probably not."

Iris peeled off the waxed paper covering the cheese.

Maggie staggered backward holding her nose. "It smells like something my dog would eat."

"Yes," said Iris. "I think you're right. And I think your sister would eat it too; we're talking total gross-out here. So – admit it. It's perfect material for the First Annual Badge Butt Gag-o-Rama. Hand me a plastic bag."

"I'm not promising I'll do this," said Maggie.

She handed Iris a small plastic bag from a box on the work-top, and Iris cut a triangle of cheese. Then, balancing it on the blade of the knife, Iris carefully slid the cheese into the bag. "Well, nobody's asking you to promise anything," Iris said in a cheerful voice. "But this way, you'll be keeping your options open. You

24

can either get him back, or not get him back. Think of this as ammunition – ammunition that gets a little deadlier while you're making your decision. And take your time! But remember, it's nothing to me! I don't care what you do. You just asked me for an idea and I gave you one, right?"

Maggie didn't answer.

"So you can either do what your father wants you to do – give Corky a taste of his own medicine – or do what your mother wants you to do – be a tell-tale. What do I care? For all I know, you liked having Corky Newton put hair in your sandwich! After all, it held the tuna together, didn't it?"

Maggie just stood there, staring at Iris.

Iris stared back. "Maggie, as far as your mother and father are concerned they have a difference of opinion – a simple difference of opinion about how a situation should be handled. They're just like any other two parents. It just so happens that they're divorced."

Maggie looked at the floor.

"Well, I mean it, Maggie! Don't worry so much about whether or not your parents agree on something. Just listen to both sides and weigh the advantages and the disadvantages. It's really not that big a deal. All we're talking about is making somebody's pants stink, right? And you're the one who has to live with the decision, so why shouldn't you make up your own mind? You're ten years old, you know – old enough to make your own decisions about Badge Butt boys!"

Then, with a flourish, Iris picked up the bag of cheese, stuck her nose into it, cleared her throat, and shook her head.

"Double-bag it," said Maggie.

Iris double-bagged the cheese, then shut the bag with a green twist tie.

"Better?"

Maggie slowly inhaled.

"It's fine," said Iris. She took a brown paper bag out of the cupboard and tossed the cheese inside. She rolled the top of the bag down and handed it to Maggie. "Put it in your pack."

They heard the vacuum cleaner stop. "Girls?" called Mrs Fuller. "What are you up to?"

"Nothing," called Iris. "Just getting a snack." She quickly reboxed the cheese and put it in the refrigerator.

"Here!" she whispered to Maggie. "Give that to me." She took the brown paper bag from Maggie, walked into the hall, and stuffed the cheese into Maggie's pack. "And," she said, "just to show you that my heart's in the right place and I'm with you all the way on this, no matter what you decide, I'm going to give you . . ." She opened up the drawer in the hat stand and fumbled through it. "This!"

She pulled out a red plastic ruler with IRIS etched on it in gold. "My Disneyland ruler! I've had it since I was a kid."

She stuck it into Maggie's pack. "You can use it to scoop out the cheese and smear it on the bench near the tetherball pole just before Badge Butt sits down." She paused. "When you're hiding behind the hedge, at lunchtime."

Maggie frowned.

"What?" said Iris. "You don't like the idea?"

"It's against the rules to go behind the hedge at lunchtime. That's considered off school grounds."

"So, what are you," said Iris, "a cop?"

Maggie said nothing.

"It's against the rules to put hair in people's sandwiches," said Iris. "And it's against the rules to extort peppermints from people."

Maggie looked thoughtful. "Well, what if Corky Newton sees me?"

"He has x-ray vision?" said Iris, "Come on. How's he going to see you behind a hedge?"

"What if he smells the cheese?"

"What if you get hit by a lightning bolt!" cried Iris. "What if an elephant falls out of the sky!" She looked into Maggie's eyes. "Do what you want. The ruler is a present, a symbol of our friendship. Now. Let's talk about the band."

The band!

Maggie had almost forgotten!

# 4

Iris slid a rhinestone necklace and several bottles of neon nail polish to one side of her desk and dumped everything that was on the seat of her chair onto the rug.

She opened the desk drawer and found a pencil and an overdue homework paper, which she turned blank side up. She wrote: keyboard – iris, lead singer – maggie, guitar – iris, and then fell off the chair onto her knees and ran her fingers up the neck of an air guitar.

"What about drums?" said Maggie.

"My parents have to order them when they get back from Europe."

"Well," said Maggie, "we might have some you could borrow. My dad used to play the bongo drums, and they're probably still around somewhere – maybe in my mum's garage. He never throws anything out."

Suddenly Maggie wished she hadn't told Iris that. If she asked about bongo drums at home, it was bound to bring up some bad subjects: her father, law school, her mother having had to sling hash. . . .

"I take that back," she said quickly. "I'd never be able to find them, and even if I could, well, they probably wouldn't be for kids."

"Well, we're not exactly kids," said Iris. She reached

into her shirt and adjusted her bra strap. Then she stood up and looked at herself sideways in the mirror. She pulled in her stomach and tucked her T-shirt into her jeans.

Iris caught Maggie's eye in the mirror. "Of course, you're still president of The Flat People's Club."

"Of course," said Maggie. She paused. "But I'm planning to ask my mum if I can have a bra."

"She should talk to my mother about it. My mum knows all about bras for flatties."

"But when will your mother be back?"

"Two weeks."

"I can't wait that long," said Maggie.

Iris ran her fingers through the hair at the top of her head. "When we have the band, I'm going to put gel in my hair and make it stick up in points at the top. And I'm going to wear my plastic headband with leopard spots."

"Good."

Iris sat back down at her desk and wrote THE PLASTIC HEAD BAND. "What do you think?"

"Of what?"

"This." Iris tapped on the paper with the pencil point. "As a name for the band."

"No," said Maggie.

"You don't like it? Why not?"

"I don't know. I guess because I don't have a plastic head. Anyway," said Maggie, "we're running out of time. We don't have to decide about the name right now. Let's talk about what we're going to wear. What *are* we going to wear?"

"Black fingerless gloves," said Iris. "And dresses. Or skirts? What about black fingerless gloves and skirts and high heeled shoes? We'll borrow stuff. Does your mother have any old clothes around?"

"I think so. Her and Dad's old clothes are packed in cardboard boxes in the garage. I could look."

"Good. And we can go to the Salvation Army for accessories. The other day I saw a cinch belt in the window with hula dancers on it."

"Really?" said Maggie.

"Yes," said Iris, pushing up her sleeves. "Now, let's see the fingerless gloves again."

"No. I've already tied them back up in my scarf, and it's way at the bottom of my pack, under the stinkola cheese."

"Why do you keep tying them up? You act like you're hiding them from somebody."

"I am," said Maggie. "My mum." She glanced out the window. "She hasn't seen them yet."

"She hasn't? I thought she gave them to you."

"Are you kidding? No! A friend of my father's bought them for me."

"Oh."

Maggie looked away. "His girlfriend, actually."

"Your father has a girlfriend?"

"I guess. Anyway," said Maggie, "I don't think my mother would like the gloves. Or my father's girl-friend for that matter."

"Why? She's a jerk?"

"Who? Samantha? No! She's not a jerk – she's a lawyer who sings in a piano bar." She paused. "She has a Porsche. A red one."

"You're making this up."

"I'm not! It's a Speedster. Anyway, the gloves would freak my mother out. Don't ask me why."

"Why?" said Iris.

"I told you, I don't know. Because she hates everything to do with my father, okay? What time is it?

I told her we'd work on our family portrait poems. They're due, you know."

"Fine," said Iris. "But first, come with me – just for a minute!"

She started up the stairs. "But be quiet," she whispered when they reached the landing.

"Why?"

"Mrs Fuller patrols this area," said Iris.

Maggie followed close behind as Iris slipped into her parents' bedroom and closed the door.

"My mother has some great old things in the back of her closet – perfect for the band! I think there are even some shoes with carved wooden heels and plastic tops. And palm trees on them!"

"Why are you whispering?" said Maggie.

"They're from Florida, from the fifties!"

Maggie looked round the room. It looked like something out of a movie set. The bed had a headboard with two cupids on it. There was a wedding picture on the wall above it in a heart-shaped silver frame.

"Want to see something?" whispered Iris. She opened the drawer of the bedside table and pulled out a metallic lace garter belt with gold bows on it. "Can you believe it! It's supposed to hold up these things." She showed Maggie some netted stockings wrapped in tissue paper.

"My mum would *never* wear that kind of stuff," whispered Maggie. "She just wears ordinary pants. Cotton pants and an athletic bra. Practical stuff. She would hate those things."

"I don't blame her," whispered Iris. "But underwear *is* my parents' business. My father had this garter belt specially designed for my mother in Paris, France."

"Well, it's gross," said Maggie. "And it's personal. Let's get out of here!"

"Why? My mum doesn't care if we see it."

"Well, my mum would!"

"No, she wouldn't," said Iris, slamming the drawer. "Why should she? We're all girls!"

She motioned to Maggie to follow her into the dressing room. "They're also importing this perfume – C'est La Vie." She picked up a tiny bottle from a group of perfume bottles arranged on a mirrored tray. "It means 'that's life!' in French. Smell." She handed the bottle to Maggie.

"Samantha also wears perfume from France," said Maggie. She twisted the glass stopper open and held it up to her nose.

"Crushed roses," said Iris.

Maggie carefully replaced the perfume on the tray. "My mum and dad used to have towels like that," she said, pointing to HIS and HERS towels that were stacked on the dressing table.

But Iris had disappeared into the bathroom.

Maggie heard her batting the toilet paper roll, and the roll whirling on the holder.

"Check out the underpants my mum gave to my dad on their anniversary," called Iris. "They're right there in his shaving kit. He thinks he's hiding them!" She giggled.

Maggie looked in the leather shaving kit and saw two plastic eyes looking back at her. They were attached to a pair of grey satin underpants with an elephant head on the front.

Iris appeared in the doorway.

"His you-know-what is supposed to go in the trunk," explained Iris. "See?" She held them up by the elastic band. "They're just for fun."

"Girls?" said Mrs Fuller from the hallway. "Is that you?"

Iris threw the elephant underpants back into her father's shaving kit and dragged Maggie by the wrist into her mother's wardrobe and shut the door.

"He *wears* those?" Maggie asked.

"Shhh!"

They heard the bedroom door open. "Iris?"

Iris and Maggie quietly pushed backwards and stood nose-to-nose between two long coats. They heard Mrs Fuller cross the carpet.

"I know you're in here."

Maggie and Iris stared at each other in the dark.

"Who's been in the perfume?"

The closet door opened.

Maggie stopped breathing.

The closet door closed – partway.

Iris frowned and listened. "She's gone," she whispered finally, and the girls stumbled out from behind the coats. Iris reached up and pulled on the light.

"There are formals in all these zipped bags," she said as they squeezed past the bags to get to the back of the wardrobe. "But they're way too long for us." Then she stood on her tiptoes and knocked a hat down from the shelf. "Try it on," she whispered. "Here." She put it on Maggie's head and patted it. "Now you look like a lift operator."

"Let's get out of here," said Maggie.

"Wait!" said Iris. She pulled a fuzzy sweater down by one sleeve. It had beaded sea shells on the front and a collar that twinkled. "What do you think?" she said, holding it against her chest.

"Of what?" said a voice behind them.

33

Maggie and Iris turned to see Mrs Fuller in the doorway.

"I was just asking Maggie whether or not she thinks Richard could have crawled up into these sweaters. He's lost."

Mrs Fuller quickly stepped back from the closet door.

"Wait!" said Iris, pushing her way past Maggie and pointing to the shaving kit. "Is that him?"

Mrs Fuller cautiously approached the shaving kit and let out a cry of alarm when she saw the elephant underwear peering out at her.

She regained her composure and quickly left the room.

"She hates hamsters," explained Iris. "And we'd better get out of here. She'll be back – with a broom."

A car horn honked.

"See? My mum's here. And we didn't get any homework done."

"*C'est la vie*," said Iris as they hurried down the stairs. "But whatever you do . . ." she said, handing Maggie her pack. "Don't forget this!"

# 5

"CHECK YOUR SHOES," said Maggie's mother as Maggie got into the car. "It smells as if you may have stepped in something."

Maggie quickly rolled down the window.

"So. How did it go?"

"Fine," said Maggie.

"Did you get anything done on your family portrait poem?"

"No."

Her mother sighed.

"Did you talk to Mrs Hall about the Newton boy?"

"No."

Her mother sighed again.

Maggie glanced down at her pack. She decided to tighten the drawstring. "But we figured out some stuff about the band. And Mum? Can we practice at our house until Iris's parents get back? Mrs Fuller won't let Iris play the keyboard in the house unless she has headphones on."

"I can't say as I blame her," said Maggie's mother with a smile. "She's a brave woman, that Mrs Fuller. I have to tip my hat to her – being in charge of Iris at her age."

"Can we?" said Maggie.

"Oh, Maggie, I don't know! What kind of a band

would it be? I hardly think Iris could be very accomplished on the keyboard. She's only just got it, hasn't she? And I can't help thinking that she just dreamed up this band idea to horse around."

"It wasn't her idea," said Maggie. "It was mine."

Her mother said nothing.

"It was!"

"Why not do something with Hilary?" said Maggie's mother. "She's such a sweet girl. And she plays the flute. I've heard she's very talented. She takes lessons, and the flute would be so pretty with your voice."

"I have a pretty voice," said Dinah from the back seat. She began singing loudly about a squirrel whisking its tail.

"Mum!" said Maggie. "It's already been decided. Iris and I are having a band. In fact, Iris *is* the band. She can make her keyboard sound like anything, including the flute. You've already said we could!"

"Don't whine!"

"You've already said we could, and all I want to know is if we can practise at our house."

"We'll see."

Maggie sighed. What was there to see? She crossed her arms on her chest and looked out of the window. All she wanted to do was have a band with Iris. What was the big deal?

They drove for a while, without speaking. They passed a billboard with a picture of a teenager drinking a Coke.

Dinah kept singing – about nuts and bushy tails.

"I'm thirsty," said Maggie. She could see the sign for the fruit stand ahead. "Can we stop at Palace of Fruit for a Coke?"

36

"We can stop at Palace of Fruit for fruit juice. And fruit," said her mother. She pulled off the road onto the gravel in front of the fruit stand. "And beets! This morning Blossom dug up all the beets and ate them. Can you believe it? But you know, after twelve years I've finally figured something out. Blossom is not a dog; she's a pig that barks."

Maggie slumped down and put her feet on the dashboard.

Her mother opened her bag and checked her wallet for cash. "If you're thirsty, let's talk juice," she said, without looking at Maggie. "Who wants juice?"

Maggie didn't answer.

"Suit yourself," said her mother. "Coming, Dinah?"

Dinah unbuckled her seat belt and opened the door. "Can I have M&M's?" she asked her mother as she got out of the car. "Sam bought me M&M's."

"No!" said her mother. "This place is filled with glorious fresh fruit from all over the state, and all anybody can think about are Cokes and M&M's!"

She marched up to the fruit stand, holding Dinah's hand.

Maggie sat in the car, staring at the signs painted with fluorescent paint: FRESH EGGS, TOMATOES, BROCCOLI – 69¢ a bunch.

Maggie watched Dinah's head appear and disappear behind the stacks of boxes as she followed her mother around under the awning. She wondered how tall Dinah would be when she finally learned to keep her mouth shut.

Maggie watched Dinah take a bag of something off a shelf and watched her mother put it back again. A few minutes later they came out, pushing a trolley with

37

two bags of produce and a purple netted bag of onions in it. Dinah was carrying a plastic bottle of something yellow.

"It's a papaya smoothie," she announced, climbing into the car.

"Sick," said Maggie. She turned around. "And shut up about Sam, would you?"

"What?"

Their mother slammed the boot and wheeled the trolley back under the awning.

"I said don't bring Sam up all the time!" whispered Maggie.

"Up where?"

"Just shut up about her, okay?" She frowned at Dinah as their mother got into the car.

"What's going on?"

"Nothing," said Maggie. She began chipping the polish off her fingernail with her thumbnail.

"You need to either repaint those fingernails or remove that polish, Maggie," said her mother as she started the car. "They're all chipped! Look at them!"

Maggie looked at her fingernails. "Can we stop at Payless and get some fluorescent nail polish? Or nail polish with glitter in it?"

"Nail polish with glitter in it! What would you want that for?"

"Sam wears nail polish with glitter in it," said Dinah.

Maggie held her breath.

"And perfume from France!"

"He wears nail polish and perfume?" said her mother. She put on the brakes and stopped in the middle of the road.

She turned around and stared at Dinah. "Who is this Sam, anyway?"

"Dad's girlfriend," said Dinah. "She's a singer!"

Maggie's heart raced.

"A girlfriend?" said her mother. She looked at Maggie. "Your father has a girlfriend – named Sam?"

"Samantha," said Maggie in a small voice.

It grew quiet for a moment.

"She's a singer?"

Maggie didn't answer.

"I thought you said Sam was a lawyer!"

"She is," said Maggie, looking away. "But she sings in a piano bar on Friday nights. Never mind the nail polish, Mum," said Maggie softly. "I don't need it."

Maggie looked down at her hands in her lap.

"Sam has a car without any roof," said Dinah. "It's a Porsche!"

Maggie looked up at her mother. "There's a pick-up truck behind us. Can we get going?"

Maggie's mother started driving slowly down the road. "Interesting," she said, "that you tried to hide it from me."

"Tried to hide what?" said Maggie. She moved her pack a little closer to the door with her foot.

"That Sam is a woman."

Maggie's mother pulled into the driveway. "You know exactly what I'm talking about, so don't play dumb. And let me tell you something, Maggie: I hate it when people try to hide things from me." She set the hand brake and turned off the engine. "Especially when it's one of my children trying to hide things from me." She took her work gloves off the dashboard and put them on. "To me it's like – lying."

Dinah stood up in the back and put her arms around her mother's neck. "And you know what else, Mum? Sam gave Maggie black lace gloves." She looked at Maggie. "Show Mum the gloves!"

39

"They're at Dad's," said Maggie. She quickly picked up her pack and got out of the car. She opened the back door for Dinah. "Let's go."

Maggie's mother took a can of pruner-sealer out of the hardware bag on the seat beside her and prised open the lid with one of her keys. She handed the keys to Maggie through the window. "I'll be in in a while. You open up."

Blossom waddled over to the car.

"Bring your papaya juice," said Maggie to Dinah. "Is it good?"

Dinah shook her head.

Blossom sniffed Maggie's pack and began slowly wagging her tail.

"Well, pick up the lid and screw it back on again. It's on the floor."

Dinah looked at the car floor. "I'm leaving it there for Perkins to play with."

"Shut up about Perkins, would you? Forget that stupid see-through dork! Just put on the lid!"

Maggie looked at her mother. "Mum? What are you looking at?"

Her mother was staring blankly through the window shield, looking at nothing. "A lawyer who sings in a piano bar," she said quietly. "So that's who he ends up with." She smiled, a little sadly. "Well, never mind!"

She got out of the car, put her arms around Maggie and Dinah, and gave them each a squeeze. "Look at the clouds rolling in! We're going to have a glorious sunset tonight!"

Maggie looked up at the sky.

It looked like rain.

# 6

ON THE KITCHEN TABLE were two loaves of homemade bread, a basket of muffins, and a pottery jug filled with yellow flowers.

"I'm thirsty," said Dinah.

"Drink your smoothie."

"I want milk."

Maggie poured Dinah a glass of milk. "Well, you spilled the beans," said Maggie. "Nice going."

"What beans?"

Maggie didn't answer. She walked into her bedroom and shut the door.

She listened for a minute. She heard Dinah humming, then talking to Perkins about muffins and flowers.

Maggie walked to the window and looked out. She could see her mother on the path – on her knees, pruning the rosebushes and putting sealer on the cuts.

Maggie opened her pack and rummaged through it until she found the knotted scarf. She untied it and took out the black lace gloves.

Then she dumped the crayons out of an empty Band-Aid box on her dresser, poked the black lace gloves inside, and stuffed the Band-Aid box in the bottom of her waste basket.

Glancing out of the window at her mother, she

fished around in her pack for the Camembert. She heard a chair scrape across the kitchen floor and then her sister's footsteps heading towards the bedroom door.

Maggie quickly dropped the cheese into the waste basket.

Dinah walked into the room, with Blossom following her. Blossom walked directly over to the basket and began pushing the papers with her nose.

"You're supposed to knock."

"Where's Mum?"

"Outside! Don't you ever pay attention?"

No, Dinah never paid attention. Maggie pulled the bag of cheese out of the waste basket and put it into her pack again, then chucked it into the wardrobe and shut the door. "Now go on!" she said to Blossom, but Blossom didn't go anywhere. She just lay on the floor in front of the wardrobe door and put her nose between her paws.

Dinah stood at the window, looking out. "Why is she cutting down all the bushes?"

"Can you get out of here?"

"Perkins spilled my milk."

"You spilled your milk. Go clean it up!"

"I can't. Perkins is making bread pudding."

Maggie jumped up. "Get a cloth!" she cried, running into the kitchen. Dinah followed her. The milk had run through the cracks between the table leaves and was dripping onto the floor.

Dinah stared at her.

Maggie stormed over to the sink and pulled a cloth from the tap where it had been hung to dry. She got down under the table and began mopping the floor with the cloth. Milk dripped on her head. "Why don't you clean up after yourself?" she shouted. "And don't tell me anything about Perkins – just shut up about Perkins. I'm not kidding, Dinah!"

But Dinah had left the room. "She isn't kidding, Perkins," Maggie heard Dinah say in the hallway.

Her mother hurried in. "What's all the commotion?"

"I've had to clean up after Dinah, as usual." Maggie threw the cloth into the sink and put her hand on the top of her head. "I bumped my head."

"Sorry," said her mother. She rinsed the cloth, rung it out, and hung it neatly on the tap.

"Dinah wet the bread," said Maggie.

"I did not wet the bed!" called Dinah from the hallway.

"Wet the *bread*!" cried Maggie.

"Calm down," said her mother. "I'll make it into stuffing."

She sat down, pulled Maggie on to her lap, and kissed the top of her head. "I don't know what I'd do without you, Maggie," she said gently. "Thank you for holding the fort when I work outside in the garden. Thank you for cleaning up after Dinah."

Maggie leaned back against her mother.

Her mother rested her chin on Maggie's shoulder. "You're getting so grown up," she whispered into Maggie's ear. "Look how big you are!"

Maggie smiled a little.

"You know," whispered her mother, "it's hard being the only parent. But with you to help me, it's almost like having another adult in the house. Really!"

"Mum?"

"What?"

"Do you really, *really* think I'm growing up?"

43

"Yes!"

"Well, Mum –"

"What?"

"Nothing."

"Tell me!"

"I was wondering – do you want me to bring in the groceries from the boot?"

"Why, yes! I forgot they were there!"

Maggie stood up. "And Mum?" She turned to her mother. "I was also wondering if –"

"If what?"

"If I – " Maggie turned and opened the dishwasher door and took out the cutlery basket. "Can have a bra?"

"A bra?" said her mother. "What for?"

"I would like to have a bra to wear," said Maggie. She began sorting knives, forks and spoons into the drawer.

"I've never even been able to get a vest on you. Now you want a brassière?"

"Yes."

"For what? What are you going to put in it?"

"Mum!" said Maggie. She set the cutlery basket on the worktop. "I'm not totally undeveloped." She unbuttoned her shirt and looked inside. "See?" She walked over to her mother, and her mother peered into Maggie's shirt.

"Well, yes, I've noticed," said Maggie's mother. "But I don't know why you need a bra – just yet."

"You wear a bra," said Maggie. "You're flat."

"I beg your pardon," said Maggie's mother. "Besides, you're ten! I'm forty! Women my age are wearing bras again, although I don't know why. They're very uncomfortable, and we never did in the sixties!"

44

"Never did what?" asked Dinah from the doorway.

Maggie quickly closed her shirt.

"Wear a bra," said her mother. "Look at the front of your shirt!"

"Wear a bra?" Dinah covered her chest with her hands. "Me?"

"No," said her mother in a gentle voice. "Not you. I was just telling Maggie that I didn't used to wear a bra and now I do. And I was pointing out that there's milk spilled down the front of your shirt."

"Iris wears a bra," said Maggie.

"Iris is in the sixth grade, Maggie. And you're in the fifth. And you don't have to do everything Iris does, do you? But if you'd like, I'll keep my eye out for something for you – perhaps a trainer bra."

"A *trainer bra*?"

"Well, just to start out with. I don't think they make an actual brassière in your size."

"Iris never said anything about starting out in a trainer bra. But she said you should ask her mother about bras. Iris's mother knows all about bras."

"Yes, I'm sure she does. She and her husband are obscene underwear importers, aren't they? And pardon me! Why would you ask me about a bra in the first place when you can talk to the experts?"

"They're gone for two weeks."

"Well, why don't you ask Iris to do a little research on the subject? You seem to think she knows everything!"

Maggie's mother turned to Dinah and held out her hand. "Want to help Mama out in the garden? Want to choose a squash?"

Dinah took her mother's hand and they went out

the door. Maggie stood at the screen, watching them. "You shouldn't have cut down the bushes," Maggie heard Dinah tell her mother.

"Jeez! Now I've got you giving me gardening tips!" Maggie heard her mother say. "Doesn't anybody think I know anything about anything? Those are roses – and I'm in charge of the roses, so mind your own beeswax!

"But for your information, shorty," she added, stopping to touch Dinah on the end of her nose, "the rose doesn't die when it gets cut down, it just redirects its energy to strengthen its roots. And comes back stronger in the spring!"

# 7

The phone rang.

It was Iris. "Listen," she said. "My Mum called from Bordeaux. She told me to look in the attic. There are some old clothes up there in a steamer trunk. My grandmother's!"

"Did you look?"

"Not yet. After supper. Also, they're going to bring back some black fingerless gloves and – get this – *some black lace tights* with no feet in them. I asked her to bring you a pair, too!"

"Did she say yes?"

"Yes, she said yes!" said Iris. "Can't you just see us? Black lace fingerless gloves and black lace tights to match. And I was wondering, do you have any hightops you could splash paint on?"

"No."

"Any old kicks whatsoever?"

"Kicks?"

"Shoes! Any old shoes, even your mother's? You could put newspaper in the toes. Then we could splash acrylic paint on them – I already know how."

Maggie lifted the kitchen curtain. "I'll ask my mum later. She's outside in the garden right now."

"Okay," said Iris. "Talk to you in a while."

"Bye," said Maggie. She hung up the phone.

47

It immediately rang again.

"Maggie?"

It was Maggie's father.

"How's it going?"

"Fine."

"Listen, there's a chance we may go fishing at Pine Meadow Lake this weekend. Samantha's got a fold-away canoe. Do me a favour, would you? Look in the garage. See if you see any fishing poles lying around – see if you see any reels."

"Okay."

"There should be three or four poles in there. And see if you can find my creel. It's a basket with a leather strap. It may have some lures and floats in it."

"Okay."

"Samantha's standing here. She says to say hello. She says she can't talk now but, but – what? She says she can't talk now, but bring your gloves this weekend and she'll sew some rhinestones on them. Oh, and what happened about the Newton kid?"

"Nothing – yet." Maggie lowered her voice. "But I have a plan."

"That's my girl! Listen, I've got a client waiting –"

"Okay, Dad."

"But about your plan –" Her father paused.

Maggie waited.

"Don't get caught."

Maggie went into her bedroom and took the Band-Aid box out of the waste basket. After all, there was no point in throwing away a perfectly good pair of fingerless gloves simply because her mother didn't want her father to have a girlfriend.

She opened the metal lid and shook out the gloves onto her bedspread. Then she stood in front of the window, pulling them on.

She saw Dinah and her mother stooping in the garden. Above them sunlight was sifting through the clouds. They were picking peas and putting them in a pot.

Maggie picked up her baton full of liquid glitter, held it against her mouth and closed her eyes, and softly began to sing.

But what about the rest of the outfit? And what about the fishing poles?

She opened her underwear drawer and tossed her gloves inside. That was a logical place to keep gloves – there was even a pair of white box-fingered gloves somewhere in the drawer. So she wasn't hiding anything from anybody.

Maggie shut the drawer and hurried out of the room. Then she hurried in again. She opened the underwear drawer and put the gloves under a stack of slips she never wore.

She went outside. She waved to her mother, but her mother didn't see her. She was on one knee in the dirt beside Dinah, pointing up to some Canada geese.

With a grunt, Maggie pulled the garage door partway up and ducked under it.

She looked around. What a mess! She saw crossed skis and ski poles but no fishing poles. How could anybody find fishing poles in such a mess? She made her way over the cardboard boxes and stacks of magazines and books and around the piles of dusty furniture to where some cardboard barrels were lined up along the wall.

She snapped open the clasp on the hoop and wiggled off the lid.

Curtains.

She closed the barrel again and opened another. On

top was a stuffed cotton dachshund – her mother's old autograph hound. She stood it on the workbench and patted its head.

Then Maggie pulled a large white plastic bag out of the barrel and undid the knot at the top. Inside was a wrinkled satin dress, pink, with pink shell buttons shaped like shells sewed down the front.

She shook it out and held it in front of her, then stepped over an apple crate so she could see her reflection in a mirror leaning against the wall.

She tossed the dress over the back of an overstuffed chair and reached into the barrel again. She pulled out two flattened alligator pumps, open-toed, with bows. She whacked them together, kicked off her shoes, and put on the pumps: definite candidates for paint splashes.

She clopped once around the barrel, then pulled out a zip bag, and unzipped it. Inside was a cashmere sweater. She flapped it out and pulled it over her head with the V in the back, then pushed up the sleeves.

Yes! It could be perfect with just a bra underneath.

Maggie rooted down through some layers of folded blouses until she came to a shirt with arrow pockets and cowboys riding on horses across the front of it. Now, where on earth had her mother got that? She unsnapped the pearl buttons and put it on over the sweater. It came down to her knees. What about a belt?

"Maggie?"

Her mother rolled the garage door the rest of the way up. "I thought you were going to bring in the groceries."

Maggie stepped out of the shadow. "How do I look?" She held open the cowboy shirt and turned once around for her mother.

"You went through my clothes barrels?"

"Well, I came in looking for fishing poles. Dad wants the fishing poles."

"You pulled out my formal? I was homecoming queen in that formal, lying in a heap on the floor. Pick it up!"

"Sorry," said Maggie. "It fell off the back of the chair."

She picked up the dress and tried to fold it.

"Give that to me!" said her mother, snatching the dress from Maggie and smacking the dust from the hem. "What else have you dragged out and stomped on?"

"Nothing," said Maggie. She took off the two alligator pumps and held them side by side in the palms of her hands. "Just these old kicks. Can I paint them?"

"These old kicks. What do you mean, these old kicks? No, you may *not* paint them. Those are alligator pumps! Your father bought those for me in London, England, before you were born! And they might be out of style, but for crying out loud, Maggie, those are alligator! Those are the real thing!"

Maggie looked down at the shoes.

When she looked up again, she saw that her mother's eyes were filled with tears.

*Oh, no!* thought Maggie. She hadn't meant to make her mother cry. She quickly put the shoes into the barrel again and took off the cowboy shirt. "I'm sorry, Mum." She pulled the sweater over her head. "Here! I'm putting everything away see?"

Her mother didn't answer. She had turned her back to Maggie and was looking out of the doorway. The sun was down. The sky was dark and low.

51

"I'm sorry about your clothes, Mum."

"I'm sorry too," said her mother. She slowly turned and looked at Maggie. "And I'm sorry I don't have a Porsche convertible. I'm sorry I don't wear French perfume. And nail polish with glitter in it."

"Please don't say that, Mum!"

"Fishing poles," said her mother. "Now he wants fishing poles. Look at this place, will you?" She moved a tyre pump across the floor with her foot. "Do you realize this garage is so full of stuff – your father's stuff – that I can't even park my car in here? I can't even walk in here without tripping over his squash rackets and bongo drums. And law books! What am I saving them for?" She kicked a lampshade against a cardboard box. "He has a brand-new house and a two-car garage with a Mercedes in it – and space enough to add . . . a Porsche," she whispered. She smiled a little and shook her head. "Why should I keep hanging on to this stuff that clutters my life?"

She looked at Maggie.

"Why?"

# 8

Iris was waiting for Maggie when she arrived at school on Tuesday morning. "You'll never guess," she called to Maggie. "I found a blue felt skating skirt with a poodle on it. And a mink collar. It's real mink, a whole one! And it's biting its own tail!"

"Gross!"

"What about you – any luck?"

"Not really."

"Not even any shoes?"

"Well, I found some alligator pumps, but they were real alligator. The real thing! So my mum said no."

"Too bad," said Iris. They headed towards the building.

Maggie noticed the principal standing at the top of the stairs, shading his eyes with one hand and surveying the yard. "By the way," she said, digging into her pack, "did you want this cheese for anything?"

"Don't tell me –" said Iris. She followed Maggie over to the dustbin. "You're chickening out?"

Maggie nodded.

She dropped the bag of cheese into the bin. "And I'm going to tell Mrs Hall about the hair sandwich."

Maggie glanced up at the staircase.

Mr Newton had gone.

Iris took the bag out of the bin. "The answer is yes," said Iris. "Yes, as a matter of fact, I might need this for something. I'm not kidding!" She took Maggie's pack and stuffed the bag inside. "So you don't mind if I keep it in here, do you?" Then she put her arm around Maggie's shoulders and strolled up the stairs and into the school, swinging the pack by one strap.

No, Maggie didn't mind if Iris kept the cheese in her backpack. In fact, she was a little honoured that Iris was carrying her backpack, since just a day or two ago she'd said that checkered backpacks were for nerds. And it felt good, walking down the hall with Iris, being pals, and going into the anteroom talking about plans for the band in loud voices so the other kids would wonder about it and wish they could be in it.

When Maggie walked into the classroom, Hilary was sharpening a lot of new pencils that said HILARY on the sides. She waved to Maggie and Maggie waved back.

Corky Newton was milling around behind the fish tank. He stopped and leered at Maggie through the glass.

She ignored him.

The bell rang. Mrs Hall walked in, wearing red lipstick and a red dress. She wrote the date on the board, took the register, and called for the clean-up captain's morning report.

Corky stood up and in a loud voice reported ants on the bookshelf, paint on the doorknob, peppermint wrappers on the floor – and an unpleasant odour in the cloakroom.

Iris and Maggie looked at each other.

Mrs Hall instructed Corky to clean the doorknob and to wait until just before lunch to check out the smell in the cloakroom. And she reminded the class that eating sweets in school was not allowed under any circumstances – at which point Corky loudly breathed air out of his nose and stared at Hilary, who was looking nervously down at her pencil, pretending that the rubber was interesting.

The morning passed slowly: reading, maths, break, spelling.

Iris raised her hand. "I can't finish my spelling. It's time for me to go to my dentist appointment."

Mrs Hall checked the clock. It was five minutes until noon. "Finish after lunch."

Iris tossed the book into her desk.

"And Corky," added Mrs Hall, "this would be a good time to check on that unpleasant smell in the cloakroom."

Iris winked as she walked past Maggie's desk. "Unpleasant smell in the cloakroom," she whispered.

Maggie opened her spelling book to a page marked DO.

She was afraid to look at Corky when he came back out. "There's a slight swampy smell," he announced. "But I couldn't identify it. It might be coming from underneath the sink."

"Thank you, Captain," said Mrs Hall.

Corky saluted. Then he said "Ha!" on the doorknob and polished it with a rag until it shone.

"It's wonderful to have such an enthusiastic clean-up captain," said Mrs Hall. "Isn't it, class?"

Nobody said anything.

The lunch bell rang. Kids opened and closed their desktops and chatted with one another as they left the room. When Maggie stopped in the cloakroom to pick up her lunch, Corky was standing by the door, watching her.

Maggie looked at him. He began whistling quietly and looking up at the ceiling. He elbowed another boy who was standing beside him, and they both turned and left the room.

All of a sudden Maggie felt something dribbling on her tights. She looked down and saw that apple juice was running out of the bottom of her lunch bag. She put the bag on the floor and looked inside.

As she suspected, the can was leaking. She took it out of the bag and turned it right side up on the floor. The foil cover on the opening at the top of the can had been partially pulled back. Her egg salad sandwich was soaked; the crust was falling off the bread. She walked over to the litter bin, threw out the sandwich, and cleaned up the trail of drips on the floor.

She looked down at her tights. One leg was stained with yellow blotches.

"Maggie?"

Maggie looked up to see Mrs Hall watching her. "My apple juice," said Maggie. "It leaked all over the place."

Mrs Hall leaned down, picked up Maggie's lunch bag, and took it over to the sink. "Well, the apple is okay," she said in a kind voice. She rinsed the apple and dried it with a paper towel. "And I think we can save the crisps." She set them on the draining board. She shut one eye and peered into the apple juice can. "Empty."

Maggie said nothing.

"Would you like half of my paté sandwich?"

"No, thank you. I'm really not hungry. I'll just have my apple and my crisps."

Mrs Hall lightly blotted the dots of apple juice from the bag of crisps.

"But thank you, anyway," said Maggie.

Mrs Hall tossed the lunch bag and the empty can into the bin. "You've got to check the seals on the tops of those little cans for leaks before you put them in your lunch."

"Right," said Maggie. "That one was peeled partway back." But she didn't add "by Corky Newton when he went to check the cloakroom."

"Well, enjoy what's left of your lunch," said Mrs Hall.

Maggie smiled a little and left the room.

Outside she saw Corky Newton leaning against the wall of the gymnasium, holding a carton of milk and a brown paper lunch bag.

She stared at him.

He stared back.

He bit off the end of the paper straw wrapper and blew it off his straw in her direction. "Did your lunch take a leak, Maggie?" he called.

Maggie's face grew hot.

He pointed at her tights. "Or did you?"

A couple of boys walked over and stood by Corky. They lowered their heads to listen to something he was telling them, then smiled. They looked at Maggie.

She quickly turned away and stormed back into the classroom.

Mrs Hall was sitting at her desk. Maggie stood in front of the teacher, holding her apple in one hand and her crisps in the other.

"Mrs Hall," she said in an unsteady voice.

"Yes, Maggie?"

"I came in because I have a problem – because I want to tell you something."

Mrs Hall smiled. "What is it Maggie?"

"I came in because I want to tell you –" Maggie paused. "That in the cloakroom, before lunch . . ."

"Yes?"

". . . I left my pack!" said Maggie quite suddenly. "I left my pack in the cloakroom before lunch, and I need it! I've got to take off my tights in the girl's room and put them in my backpack. There's apple juice all over them. And I need to put these in my pack" – she held up the apple and the crisps – "to carry them out."

"Good idea," said Mrs Hall. "That's it?"

"That's it," said Maggie. She went into the cloakroom, took her pack out from under the coatrack, and dropped her apple and crisps into it. Then she went into the girl's room across the hall from her classroom and took off her tights, balled them up, and stuffed them into her pack.

And she hurried outside to the picnic tables.

"Want to sit down?" asked Hilary. She moved over, making a space for Maggie on the bench and patting it. "Where's your lunch?"

Maggie didn't answer. She looked over to where Corky Newton was standing.

"That stinks!" Corky was shouting to a little kindergarten boy holding a cupcake.

The boy smelled the cupcake and Corky shoved it into his nose.

"Sorry!" shouted Corky. "Really – sorry! It was an accident!"

Maggie glanced over her shoulder at the teacher on yard duty. "Save me a place, would you?" she said to Hilary.

Then she slipped behind some bushes that were growing by the side of the cafeteria building. And when the coast was clear she moved from shrub to shrub until she got to the place where the hedge around the school yard began.

She stooped down and quickly made her way along the pavement behind the hedge. *I can't believe I'm doing this*, she said to herself. She stopped and peered through a gap in the shrubbery. She was directly behind the bench near the tetherball pole.

And Corky Newton was walking toward her!

Maggie fumbled through her pack until she found the stinky cheese. She dumped the plastic bag out of the paper bag and onto the pavement.

She untwisted the wire and gagged.

Then Maggie took Iris's Disneyland ruler out of the bottom of her pack. She scooped the cheese onto the end of the ruler and scooted to where the back of the bench almost touched the hedge – and waited.

Corky was kicking a pebble towards the bench. Maggie saw him stop for a minute to check the bottom of one shoe. Then he kicked the pebble one more time, and it bounced into the dry leaves under the hedge, almost hitting Maggie.

Maggie held her breath.

Corky took two long strides and turned around to sit on the bench. And when he turned, Maggie reached through the gap in the hedge and smeared the cheese from the ruler onto the bench slats.

*Hallelujah!* thought Maggie as Corky sat on the cheese. He put his bag of lunch and carton of milk on the bench beside him and took a deep breath, slowly, through the nose.

Maggie watched through the leaves as he checked the bottom of his other shoe, then leaned way over and looked between his knees at the ground underneath his feet.

She saw his face, upside down. His cheeks were red; his eyes were bulging.

*God, don't let him see me,* prayed Maggie.

Corky sat up and sniffed the air. He turned for a moment and looked in Maggie's direction.

Maggie didn't dare move. She had to breathe so slowly and quietly she could barely get enough air. Get Corky Newton back, Maggie had thought. What a great idea. But what if he kicked her butt? Maggie's father hadn't got around to explaining about that. Of course he hadn't; what did he know about the problems kids had in public school? He'd gone to prep school in Vermont! Next time she'd listen to her mother!

Corky unrolled the top of his lunch bag and looked in. Then he opened his milk carton and brought it close to his nose, smelling the milk. He leaned down and poured the milk onto the dirt under the bench, closed the carton, put it on the ground, and popped it with his foot.

He kicked the carton under the bench.

Corky took his sandwich out of the bag and slowly unwrapped it. He lifted the corner of the top piece of bread and peered at the slice of bologna covered with yellow mustard. He lifted the bread up closer. Then he smelled the slice of bologna, flopped the bread back onto the sandwich, balled the sandwich up in the waxed paper, and rolled it under the bench.

There was a blob of mustard on the end of his nose.

Corky took a peach out of the bottom of his lunch bag and poked at a rotten spot on it with his finger. He sighed loudly. Then he took a few bites from the other side of the peach and, looking over his shoulder to make sure that the yard duty teacher wasn't watching, chucked the peach over the hedge. He walked over to the tetherball. He rolled his tongue backward, held it between his teeth, and socked the ball. He slammed it again. The ball wound round the pole, round and round, faster and faster.

*Yikes!* thought Maggie. She could see the cheese smeared across the tin sheriff's badge pinned to Corky's back pocket. *Let me out of here*, she thought. She grabbed the strap of her back pack and, holding it against her chest, duckwalked all the way along the hedge without looking back.

She stood up and brushed off when she reached the side of the cafeteria. Then she went bush by bush again until she approached the picnic tables.

She casually walked towards Hilary.

"Where did you go?" asked Hilary in a loud voice.

"Nowhere," said Maggie.

"You did too."

Maggie sat down and, whistling quietly, rooted through her backpack. She found her crisps and opened the corner of the bag with her teeth.

"You're not supposed to go behind the buildings," said Hilary.

"What are you, a cop?" said Maggie.

Hilary said nothing.

Maggie ate her crisps. She rubbed her apple on her trousers and took a bite.

"P.U.!" she heard someone scream. It was the kindergarten boy with icing on his nose. "P.U.!" he shouted again, and pointed to Corky Newton, who was waddling towards the school.

"What happened?" said Hilary.

"I don't know," said Maggie. "I guess Corky Newton pooped in his pants."

Hilary's eyes grew rounder. They watched him go up the steps and into the building.

Maggie took two bites of her apple, one right after the other. Apple juice ran down her chin, and she wiped it with her arm and smiled.

She began humming a little song and moving her head back and forth cheerily, eating her apple and drumming the fingers of one hand on the top of the table.

She could hardly wait to tell Iris!

And she could hardly wait to tell her dad!

# 9

"CORKY'S IN THE OFFICE," said Iris. "He has an – odour problem."

A few kids giggled.

"A major one."

Iris handed Mrs Hall a pass from the school secretary. Then she spun around and did thumbs-up to Maggie, but Maggie pretended she didn't see.

A figure appeared behind the glass window in the door. Mrs Hall went to the door and opened it. She turned to the class and said, "It's the principal. Kindly take out some work to do until I return."

Mrs Hall went just outside the door and partly closed it, then stuck her head back in and frowned at the class. "What are you waiting for?" she said. "Get busy."

Maggie quickly took out her social studies workbook. She leafed through the book until she got to the page that had CORRECT THIS PAGE written at the top in red pencil.

She glanced over at the door, at the two shadows that were moving behind the glass.

She rubbed out an answer that was written on a line with a red mark beside it. What was the importance of indigo to the colonists? How was she supposed to know? She didn't even know what indigo was! She went on to the next red mark and read the question again and again without thinking about what it was asking.

The doorknob turned, and Mrs Hall walked into the room. "Is this your ruler, Iris?" she said, holding up a red plastic ruler with IRIS etched on it – and with the end wrapped in newspaper.

Maggie slumped down in her chair.

"My ruler?" said Iris.

Mrs Hall frowned at her. "Yes. I'm asking you – is this your ruler?"

"Does it say IRIS on it?"

"Yes."

"Does it say DISNEYLAND?"

"Yes."

Iris groaned.

"May I speak with you for a moment – outside?"

"Wait," said Maggie in a small voice. She stood up, brushed off her skirt, and slowly walked to the front of the room. "It's my ruler. Iris gave it to me."

"Iris gave this to you?"

"Yes."

"When did Iris give this to you?"

"She gave it to me yesterday," squeaked Maggie.

Mrs Hall looked at Iris. "Did you?"

Iris shrugged.

Mrs Hall took off her glasses and pinched the bridge of her nose, with her eyes shut. "Well, did you or didn't you?"

Iris didn't answer.

Mrs Hall walked over to the window, opened it, and put the ruler outside on the ledge.

Then she closed the window. "I think Mr Newton would be interested in talking to both of you," she said in a stern voice.

She scribbled a note to the principal and handed it to Iris. Iris and Maggie quickly left the room and walked down the hallway to the principal's office.

"We're busted," whispered Iris. She put her hand out in front of Maggie to make her stop walking. "What happened?"

Maggie looked down at the floor. "I must have forgotten to pick it up. I must have left it on the pavement."

They walked into the office. Iris gave the note to the school secretary, Mrs Puntz. "You may go in," the secretary said crisply, handing the note back to Iris. "Show it to Mr Newton." She waved her hand in the air to indicate that they should get going.

The principal's door was open. He was sitting at his desk, his hands folded on a large green blotter with black triangles at the corners. "May I help you?" he said to Maggie and Iris.

Iris gave him the note. He frowned as he read it.

Corky was standing near the windows, wearing a pair of light blue corduroy bell-bottom trousers that were three or four inches too short for him. The fly was pinned shut with two safety pins. He was holding a large brown paper bag, rolled closed at the top. Maggie and Iris looked at him.

"Nice floods, Corky," said Iris.

"What?" said Mr Newton.

"I was just saying that Corky looks nice in those trousers. I like how they're kind of short – kind of half-mast," said Iris. "And I like how they're bell-bottoms! He looks like a dude."

She glanced at Corky, and he scowled at her.

Iris elbowed Maggie. Then she slowly breathed in. "Corky!" she said, pinching her nose. "Did you squeeze the cheese?"

"What?" said Mr Newton.

"I was wondering if Corky . . . let a fluffy."

"Sit down!"

Maggie quickly sat down in a large oak chair and folded her hands in her lap.

Iris dragged another large oak chair away from Corky and sat down, with her arms on the armrests and her legs stretched out and crossed at the ankles.

"Sit up, Iris."

She sat up. "Could we open a window? I need some fresh air."

Mr Newton didn't answer. And the room grew very quiet. He took a pen out of the plastic pen holder in his shirt pocket and began clicking the clicker.

Maggie looked down at her hands.

"There are a lot of students here at Franklin Middle School," said Mr Newton. He looked at Maggie. "Young lady? Do you know how many students go to this school?"

Maggie politely said no.

He raised one eyebrow and looked at Iris.

She shook her head.

"Well. There are two fourth grades. There is one fourth-fifth combination." He leaned back in his chair and looked at the ceiling. "Let's see."

"Two fifth grades!" said Iris.

"Don't interrupt." He paused. "There are two fifth grades. There is one fifth-sixth combination. And there is one sixth grade. Right?"

Maggie nodded.

Iris shrugged.

"Right?" said Mr Newton to Iris.

Iris shrugged again. "I guess so."

Mr Newton clicked his pen a few more times and stared at Iris.

She tapped her fingers on the armrests of the chair.

"Well, I'm telling you. That's how many classes we have at Franklin Middle School. Sit up, Iris! I told you, sit up! Sit like a lady!"

Maggie tried to adjust her position, but her legs were stuck to the seat of the chair.

"Gee, Uncle Gerald, that must be almost three hundred students!" said Corky to Mr Newton. "That's a lot!"

Iris stared at Corky.

"Yer dern tootin' that's a lot," Mr Newton said to Corky in a serious voice. He rapidly clicked his pen. "And it's quite a job, keeping that many kids in line."

He eyeballed Maggie, then Iris.

"You're getting ink on your arm," Iris told him.

He looked down at the little dots of ink that he'd accidentally drawn on his arm while clicking his pen. "It's my job to worry about my pen, not your job," he told Iris. "And it's also my job to run this school and see that the school environment is conducive to learning. *Therefore*," he said, raising his voice and looking at Maggie, who jumped, "it's my job to set out rules that need to be followed. And it's your job to –?"

"To follow them," Maggie said in a very high voice.

"Did you follow the rules at lunch today?"

She looked down at her hands in her lap. "No."

"Well, would you like to tell me what rules you broke?"

Iris slowly moved her shoe over so that it touched Maggie's shoe, and nudged her.

"What rules I broke?" said Maggie.

Her stomach ached. Her chest ached. She couldn't fill her lungs with air.

"Yes," said Mr Newton. "In other words, what led

to Mrs Puntz finding the ruler that Iris gave you – *off the school grounds* – when she slipped on a peach and fell into the hedge on her way to the mailbox at the corner?"

Iris closed her eyes and shook her head.

"I went behind the hedge," whispered Maggie.

"Speak up."

"I went behind the hedge," said Maggie.

"Look at me when I talk to you and when you talk to me," said Mr Newton in a stern voice.

Maggie looked up. She began rubbing her cheek and her chin with one hand.

"Anything else?"

"I put cheese on the bench so Corky would sit in it."

Mr Newton looked at Maggie for a long time, and Maggie kept looking at Mr Newton. Mr Newton's face got blurry, and when Maggie blinked, two tears rolled down her cheeks.

"What do you think your mother will say about this, Maggie?"

Maggie shrugged and wiped her tears away with the backs of her hands. "She won't like it," she managed to say, although her mouth was trembling so badly she could barely talk.

"No. I would certainly say she won't."

Maggie wondered if he was going to ask her what her father would think. Didn't he know she had a father? She had a father!

Two more tears rolled down her cheeks, and a little snort came out of her, from out of somewhere. And for just a moment Maggie thought she might need to cover her face with her hands.

"It was my idea," said Iris calmly. "I thought the whole thing up – and I gave Maggie the ruler so she could do it."

Mr Newton looked from Maggie to Iris.

"No, it wasn't!" cried Maggie.

But Mr Newton ignored her. "So it was your idea. I could have guessed you'd have put her up to this."

"That's right," said Iris. "I planned it. I gave her the cheese. I told her how to go behind the hedge."

She turned and made cross-eyes at Corky Newton, then screwed up her face and struck out her tongue at him.

"Turn around!" shouted Mr Newton, his face growing very red.

Iris whirled around. "Look," she told him, pointing to Corky with her thumb. "That clown over there thinks it's fun to trash people's lunches – to put hair in people's sandwiches."

"And to open up the seal on my apple juice can," said Maggie in an unsteady voice. "And to pick up girls' ponytails and look underneath!"

Mr Newton's face relaxed, and he smiled a little at Maggie. "Boys will be boys," he told her. He looked over at Corky and winked. "I used to pick up pony tails too."

"I'm not surprised," said Iris with a sneer. "Some things seem to run in families. Did you also used to extort candy from people? Your nephew over there extorts candy from people while pretending to be doing his job as clean-up captain!"

"I do not!" said Corky.

"You do too, you liar."

"That's *enough*!" shouted Mr Newton. He stood up. "I've heard *enough* from you, young lady!"

He put his hands on his hips and looked at Corky.

"Corky," said Mr Newton. "Have you ever abused the privileges of your job as clean-up captain at

Franklin Middle School, *ever?*"

"No."

Mr Newton cleared his throat. "Have you ever tampered with anybody's lunch at Franklin Middle School, *ever?*"

"No."

"Then you may give that paper bag to Maggie and tell her to have her mother wash your trousers and return them to school."

Corky walked over and dropped the paper bag on Maggie's lap. He looked at her for a moment, then forced a smile. "Tell your mother to wash them and return them to the school."

Maggie stared at the bag.

Corky turned to Mr Newton. "But Uncle Gerald, is the badge washable?"

"Well, not in the washing machine. But I'm sure Maggie's mother can rinse it off. And shine it. Now, you are excused."

Mr Newton slipped a piece of memo paper into his typewriter and typed a note for Corky to return to class. He pulled it from the typewriter and signed his name at the bottom.

"Is there anything you would like to say to Corky about this incident?" he said to Maggie.

Maggie looked at Corky and lowered her eyelids half-way.

"Sorry," she said.

Corky stared at her. "Just don't let it happen again, okay?" He turned to leave the room, and as he turned, Iris edged closer to Mr Newton's desk and stepped on the back of Corky's sneaker and gave him a flat tyre.

"Oh, sorry," said Iris to Corky. But when he leaned

down to fix his shoe, she leaned down with him and whispered, "For this you die."

"Iris?" said Mr Newton. "For instigating a younger student to violate school rules at lunchtime you will be asked to sit in the office during lunch break tomorrow."

"No problem."

"What?"

"Yes, Mr Newton."

"Maggie?" said Mr Newton. "For leaving the school grounds during the lunchtime and wilfully dirtying the clothing of a fellow student you will be asked to sit in the office every day at lunch recess for the rest of the week."

"Yes, Mr Newton," said Maggie.

"You will eat your lunches and remain seated in the chairs by the wall. Mrs Puntz will assign you some office work if necessary. So be prepared to be cheerful little junior secretaries."

He tore a pink paper from his memo pad and spun it up into position in his typewriter, typed a few words and spun it out again. "Your pass to class," he said, signing it with a flourish. He handed it to Maggie and ushered them out of his office. "Mrs Puntz," he said in a loud voice, "these young ladies need office assignments at lunchtime tomorrow."

"Well, the lost-and-found box needs tidying up and going through. It's filled with things from over the years. I'll pull it out of the cupboard. You good tidiers?"

Maggie smiled and nodded.

Iris said nothing.

"Good day, ladies!" said Mr Newton. "And let's not have any repeats of today's shenanigans!"

Maggie and Iris walked out of the office and down the hall.

When they were gone, Mr Newton quickly took a Kleenex out of the box on his desk, spat on the tissue twice and rubbed the ink dots off his arm.

# 10

MAGGIE'S MOTHER SLID a rubber poncho out from underneath the workbench in the garage. "What did I tell you about listening to your father? Step back! This is crawling with centipedes!" She carried the poncho over to the dustbin on the end of a hockey stick. "I told you! If you have a problem at school with another student, tell Mrs Hall! Didn't I tell you that?"

Maggie said nothing.

"Didn't I?"

"Yes. I said I'm sorry."

"Well, it makes me mad, Maggie! And as far as I'm concerned, you can call your father at the office and tell him to come over here and get those stinky designer blue jeans and wash them himself – unless Camembert cheese would ruin the filter on his computer-operated washing machine. Heaven forbid! We wouldn't want that to happen, would we?"

"I said I would wash them, Mum. I've already scraped most of the cheese off with a stick, and I'm going to spray them with the hose. I came in because – I want you to teach me how to run the washing machine."

"Teach you how to run the washing machine," mumbled Maggie's mother. "Like I have nothing else to do, right? Well let me tell you something," she said, tossing a fat green law book onto a stack of fat green law books in the corner. "Everything goes! Friday, come hell or high water, this stuff is going to be out of here."

"Mum! How do I run the washing machine?"

Maggie's mother moved her hair away from her eyes with one hand. "Listen to me," she said. "Concentrate. Put in one cup of detergent, then push the knob in, turn it in a circle until you get to number three, and pull it out. But do it first! So the washer can be filling with soapy water while you're hosing off the cheese. Then drop the jeans in. Tell me – who in their right mind would save this?" She held up a record album that looked as if somebody had taken a bite out of the edge. "He's been saving this since 1969!"

She sailed it through the air out of the garage, onto the driveway. "And don't you take any more of your father's advice, Maggie Hunter! The guy wore knee socks. He played squash."

"You've already told me this –"

"But you didn't listen to me, did you?"

Maggie began to walk away.

"Don't turn your back on me when I'm talking to you."

"Sorry!"

"I'm asking you: What would he know about dealing with these rural hooligans? He thinks pounding on a drum in a public park with a bunch of bums is 'putting his hand on the pulse of the common man.' Do you know what I was doing then? Waiting tables! To help pay his tuition so that he could become a lawyer. And divorce me! And have a girlfriend with a convertible Porsche!"

"Mum," said Maggie, "I don't understand. What

does cheese on the back of somebody's blue jeans have to do with hooligans or bongo drums? Or Samantha?"

"Nothing!" shouted her mother.

Maggie quickly left the garage. She went into the basement of the house and poured three cups of detergent into the washing machine, turned the dial in a circle until she came to number one, and pulled it out.

Then she hurried out of the basement door.

"Dinah!" she hollered.

Dinah was wheeling a doll's pram down the path.

"Did you move the jeans that were on the lawn?"

"No."

Blossom walked slowly down the path towards Dinah and collapsed beside the doll's pram.

Dinah patted the dog's head.

Blossom yawned.

"You need to brush your teeth," said Dinah to Blossom.

"There they are," said Maggie. "Now who dragged those jeans over there?" She picked up the hose and pulled it across the lawn.

Maggie leaned down with her hands on her knees and stared at the trousers. "Uh-oh," she said. She got down on her knees and spread out the jeans for a better look. "Did Blossom drag these over here?"

"Yes," said Dinah.

Maggie raced into the garage, her heart pounding.

"Mum!" she shouted. "Blossom's torn the pocket off Corky's jeans!"

Her mother was sweeping the floor. "I knew it would be impossible to accomplish anything out here," she said. "And great. Just great, Maggie. Now Corky Newton has to be provided with a new pair of jeans."

She leaned on the broom handle and closed her eyes.

"But Mum," said Maggie, bringing her hand to her throat. "I think Blossom's eaten the pocket!"

Her mother opened her eyes. "Why are you just standing there?"

Maggie ran outside.

A minute later Maggie came back in, dragging Blossom by the collar. "The pocket isn't out there anywhere!" she gasped, pulling the dog across the cement into the middle of the garage. She prised Blossom's jaws open and peered into her mouth.

"And it isn't in here," Maggie said, looking down Blossom's throat. She let go of the dog's jaw and smelled her hands.

She stared at Blossom.

"Bring her into the house," said her mother. "We've got to call the vet."

Dinah followed them in, singing "Perkins is making bubbles in the basement" again and again, making up a tune as she went along.

"Does he have a trouser pocket with him?" asked Maggie.

"No, Perkins doesn't have a trouser pocket with him!" shouted her mother. She grabbed the phone book from the kitchen worktop and began flipping through the yellow pages.

When she got to the $V$'s, she ran her finger down the list of names. "555-9984," she whispered, and pushed the buttons of the telephone.

"Yes," she said when somebody answered. "I need to talk to the vet. Yes. No. No, I need to talk to the vet." She covered the receiver with her hand. "Now I have to listen to canned music. They put me on hold and make me suffer through – hello? Yes, Dr Montgomery. Our dog – Blossom? She's eaten a trouser pocket." She frowned. "Just a minute, please." She looked at Maggie. "Why are you waving your hands at me?"

"And a little tin sheriff's badge," said Maggie.

"How little?" she said to Maggie.

Maggie measured an inch and a half in the air with her fingers and whispered, "Shaped like a star."

Her mother groaned. "And a tin badge about an inch and a half across, shaped like a star."

Maggie walked into the living room. "Wait!" she shouted. "She's gagging up something on the rug!"

"Just a minute!" cried Maggie's mother into the receiver.

"Hooray!" shouted Maggie, running into the kitchen. "She's sicked up the pocket!"

"Lucky me," said her mother to the vet. "The dog has apparently vomited up the pocket on my hand-woven silk rug. The badge? I don't know. Maggie make sure that the sheriff's badge is there."

Maggie raced back into the living room.

"My daughter is checking," said Maggie's mother into the telephone.

Maggie walked back into the kitchen. "She's eaten it again."

"She's eaten it again," Maggie's mother reported to Dr Montgomery. "Now what?"

She made a sour face. "Yes, I realize that tin is sharp."

She listened shaking her head. "You really think that's necessary? It's already gone down twice and up once without any problems." She put one hand on her hip and began tapping her foot.

Then she frowned. "No, I can't imagine what tin star points might do to a dog's oesophagus – or a dog's intestines. Blood? I don't think so. . . ."

Maggie's legs felt weak. She sat on the edge of a kitchen chair and stared at her mother.

Her mother brought her hand up to her heart and rolled her eyes at Maggie. "Yes, of course we're attached to this animal," she said in a serious voice. She lightly patted her chest with the palm of her hand. "We'll be right there," she said, and hung up.

She pointed at Maggie. "Don't you cry! We've got ten minutes to get there! Find the leash!"

Maggie's mother stormed into the living room. "Good going, you jerk!" she said to Blossom, who lowered her ears and thumped her tail.

"And sick!" she said, looking at a pink and yellow gooey spot on the rug. "Bloody Blossom sick on the rug my father brought me back from China!"

"Mum!" whispered Maggie, struggling to gain control of her voice. "Will Blossom be okay?" Her chin was trembling. "Please! Say Blossom will be okay!"

But Maggie's mother didn't hear her. She was pushing Blossom out the door. "Never mind the leash!" she shouted. "Get in the car!"

# 11

THE NEXT MORNING at a little past eight, Maggie's mother dropped Maggie off in front of the school. Maggie stood on the pavement and waved until her mother drove away.

Then she slowly walked across the yard. There was an exhilarating chill in the air: the sky was blue, the clouds were high and feathery. But Maggie didn't feel exhilarated; she felt pooped.

"What's the matter with you?" called Iris.

Maggie glanced over her shoulder to make sure her mother's car was out of sight. "Me? Why?"

"You're looking a little – weird, that's all."

Maggie sighed. "I'm worried about Blossom. She had to have emergency stomach surgery."

"Really?" said Iris. "They carved her open, like a pumpkin?"

"Don't say that," said Maggie. "It makes me woozy to think about it."

"Sit down," said Iris.

Maggie sat on the bench, and Iris sat beside her. "She ate the pocket off Corky's jeans. It had the sheriff's badge on it. I guess she smelled the cheese." She paused. "The vet's bill is going to be eight hundred and sixty dollars."

"Wow."

"The worst thing is that . . ." Maggie closed her eyes. "Blossom might not be able to bark anymore. They had to shove a tube down her windpipe during surgery. It damaged her vocal cords."

"Boy," said Iris. She linked her arm through Maggie's arm.

"The vet says she sounds more like a duck than a dog. He doesn't know if it's permanent. It's too early to tell."

Maggie looked up at Iris. "I just hope she's going to be okay," she whispered.

"She'll be okay," said Iris. "The vet will fix her up. For eight hundred and sixty dollars, Blossom should come out better than new."

"My mum is so mad at my dad, you wouldn't believe it. She's making him pay the bill. And she's making him take care of Blossom when the vet releases her too. Someone has to make sure she doesn't scratch her stitches. And Mum told Dad to go over and give Corky Newton's mother fifty-four dollars to buy him new trousers!"

"Boy," said Iris. She clasped her hands on top of her head. "Fifty-four dollars? Couldn't you just have asked the vet for the pocket and asked your mother to sew it back on the trousers?"

"Apparently that's what my dad suggested – just before my mum hung up on him."

"Oh," said Iris.

Maggie sighed.

"And when they were arguing on the telephone, my mum burned a hole in the rug her father brought her from China."

Iris looked over at Maggie.

"She was drying a sick mark that she'd washed with the lamp."

"She washed a sick mark with a lamp?"

"No. She washed the mark with Woolite. She took the shade off the lamp and put the light bulb close to the rug to dry it, so it wouldn't get mouldy."

"Oh."

"And the light bulb burned a hole in the rug."

"Oh."

"Our only nice rug – the one with roses on it. It's silk. My grandfather brought it all the way back from China for her, and now there's a hole burned in the middle of it. Can you believe it?"

"No."

"Even Dinah's mad at me," said Maggie. "She says I squashed Perkins in the door of the vet's office. She says I broke his ankle. It's not funny!"

"I'm not laughing," said Iris.

"You're thinking of laughing."

Iris said nothing.

"Have I already told you I flooded the basement by putting three cups of detergent in the washing machine instead of one?"

"No," said Iris. "I don't think it's funny," she told Maggie. "Really."

"The worst thing," said Maggie, looking away, "the worst thing is that Mum said I can't have a band with you."

"How come?"

"Oh, I don't know," said Maggie. "She says we just cooked up the band so we could horse around together – that we're more interested in dressing up than in making music."

"Well," said Iris, "she might have a point there."

"And she says that you're an instigator. That you're too fast for me. That you get me to do things I wouldn't

81

ordinarily do. She says she's tired of your shenanigans. And she says she's tired of your – mouth."

"Oh," said Iris.

Maggie stood up and picked up her things from the
bench. "My mum doesn't want me playing with you
for a while. I'm sorry! She's just really mad at you!"

"She'll get over it," said Iris.

They went into the school and into the classroom.
The morning passed. And at break Maggie went to the
library by herself instead of playing handball in the
playground with Iris like she usually did.

"Hello, Maggie," said Mrs Williams, the librarian.
"Can I help you find something?"

"Oh, I don't know."

The librarian gestured toward the shelves. "Let's
look." They strolled together across the carpet. "Tell
me what you're interested in, now that you're in the –
what? The fifth grade?"

"Yes," said Maggie.

"Time flies," said Mrs Williams. "I remember when
you were just a little bitty girl who couldn't even see
over my desk."

Maggie smiled a little.

"Well, this year I'm interested in dogs," she said.
"And I wonder . . .would you have any books about
dog – bodies?"

"Dog bodies?"

"You know, like about dog stomachs and dog vocal
cords. That kind of thing."

"Dog stomachs and dog vocal cords," said the
librarian. "Let's see. Animal anatomy . . ." She gave
Maggie a puzzled look and slowly shook her head. "I
don't think we have anything that specific about dog
anatomy. But I might be able to call the district

librarian and have one sent over."

Maggie felt a wave of nausea, thinking about intestines and vocal cords.

"No, don't do that," said Maggie. "It's just for – a report I have to do, for Mrs Hall. For science! And it's not due for a long time. But I wouldn't mind reading a book about a band."

"A book about a band. A marching band?"

"A rock band. I'm planning to be a rock singer when I grow up."

"Good for you," said the librarian. She frowned at the ceiling and pinched her chin. "Ha!" she said. "I know." She took Maggie's hand and led her to a shelf of books under the window. She moved her fingers across the bindings. *The Ella Fitzgerald Story*," she read, tipping the book down from the shelf. "Ever heard of Ella Fitzgerald?"

"No."

She put the book into Maggie's hands.

"This isn't a book about a rock band but it's about a singer. A jazz singer, Maggie. A real star! And knowing you, you'll like it."

They walked together to the check-out desk. The librarian tapped on an announcement that was thumb tacked to the bulletin board. "And you be careful to remember, Maggie: tryouts for the choir are this Friday. Some of the best rock stars get started in elementary school choirs, so don't forget."

"They do?"

The librarian nodded. She took a card out of the paper envelope glued to the inside cover of *The Ella Fitzgerald Story* and stamped it with a rubber stamp.

"I was thinking of having a band with Iris," Maggie said.

The librarian gave Maggie the book. "That's a good idea!"

"But it didn't work out. My mum changed her mind because – never mind."

"Tell me!"

"Because – well, you know Iris."

"Yes," said the librarian, "I do know Iris."

"Well, Iris and I got in trouble with the principal because I did something to Corky Newton."

The librarian's face lit up. "What did you do to Corky Newton? Never mind. You don't have to tell me." She moved closer to Maggie and whispered, "But I bet he deserved it!"

Maggie looked at the librarian for a long time. "Anyway," she said, "the band – it wouldn't have been much of a band. We were just using it as an excuse to get dressed up. And Iris – she's not particularly good on the keyboard."

"Oh, I don't know about that," said the librarian. "Didn't Iris once take piano lessons?"

Maggie shrugged.

She looked at the floor. "I was going to be the lead singer. I even have black lace fingerless gloves to wear! But actually, I don't have a very good voice."

"Now, Maggie. That's not true," said the librarian. "You've been humming away in this library for years, and I've noticed your voice! You've got a lovely soprano voice. Why do you think I want you to try out for choir?"

Maggie didn't answer.

"So I'll see you Friday, okay? And bring along your friend Iris. I can always use a loudmouth in the alto section. And bring those fingerless gloves! I've never seen black lace fingerless gloves. Where in the world did you get them?"

"A friend of my father's named Sam gave them to me."

"That was nice of him," said the librarian.

The bell rang, and Maggie waved and walked out of the library, but a few seconds later she went back. "Mrs Williams," she said.

The librarian turned around.

"I don't really have to do a report on veterinary medicine. And my father's friend Sam? She's a woman."

"And Mrs Williams?" she said in an unsteady voice. "Do you think my dog, Blossom, is going to be okay?"

"Your dog, Blossom?" She pulled a chair forward for Maggie. "Sit down. What's the matter with your dog, Blossom?"

"They carved open her stomach last night – like a pumpkin."

"They did?" cried Mrs Williams. "Why?"

"She ate Corky Newton's clean-up captain badge. It cut her throat."

Mrs Williams pulled a chair up close to Maggie's and sat down. "Is she at the vet's?"

"Yes," said Maggie quietly.

"Well, how is she today?"

Maggie shrugged. She wiped a tear. "It was too early to call when I came to school this morning."

"Listen," said Mrs Williams, taking Maggie's hand. "Come into my office this minute. We'll phone your mother. She must have heard something by now."

She handed Maggie the receiver. "What's the number?"

Maggie told her the number, and the librarian punched the buttons and waited.

"Nobody home," said Maggie. "But she might be

85

out cleaning the garage. Unless –'' She handed Mrs Williams the phone. ''You don't think anything – bad has happened do you? To Blossom?''

''Let's call your father,'' said Mrs Williams.

They rang his number, and the receptionist answered. ''Law offices,'' the receptionist said. ''May I help you?''

''I would like to talk to my dad.''

''Mr Hunter? One moment, please.''

The phone clicked. ''Hello?'' said Maggie's father.

''Dad?'' said Maggie.

Mrs Williams patted Maggie's back and tiptoed to the doorway.

''Is Blossom going to be okay?''

''You bet she is,'' he said in a cheerful way. ''She's fit as a fiddle. I just spoke to Dr Montgomery. And Samantha's going to pick her up this afternoon.''

Maggie wiped her eyes on her shirt sleeve, and her chin began to tremble. ''Good,'' she squeaked. She covered her mouth with her hand and squeezed her eyes closed.

''Maggie?''

Mrs Williams took the phone. She put her arm around Maggie's shoulder and pulled her close. ''Mr Hunter? What's happened? This is Henrietta Williams, the school librarian. I've got a very upset little girl here.''

''No! I'm fine!'' cried Maggie. She took the phone again. ''I was worried,'' she told her father, curling the phone cord. ''I thought she might be – dead.''

''Dead! Are you kidding? The vet said she's acting like a puppy. And she's barking her head off.''

Maggie wiped her nose on her arm. ''Does she sound okay?''

"Marvellous!" said her father. "We'll call you tonight and have her quack into the phone!"

Mrs Williams handed Maggie a tissue, and Maggie blew her nose. "I'd better go," she said.

"Okay. Well, see you, sweetie," said her father. He paused. "Is your mother still in orbit?"

Maggie glanced at the librarian. "Yes."

"Well, she'll get over it. Did you find the fishing poles?"

"They're broken in half."

"Really? How could that have happened?"

Maggie said nothing.

"Actually broken in half? All of them?"

"She's pretty mad, Dad. A lot of your stuff is going to the dump."

Mrs Williams strolled out of the room.

"And you know the rug that Grandpa gave her? There's a hole burned in it – in the middle of one of the roses, right were Blossom threw up."

"You're not serious! The dog sick burned a hole in the rug?"

"No, the lamp did, when Mum was trying to dry it. It's wrecked."

"Oh, no," said her father. "It isn't wrecked. The rose can be rewoven – good as new, or better. Don't worry so much. The rose can be rewoven, and the dog is fine. She eats like a horse and barks like a duck and looks like a pig. What more do you want? Now go back to class."

# 12

"Done, girls?" said mrs puntz after Maggie and Iris had crumpled up their brown paper bags and put them in the bin.

"Yes," said Maggie.

"Well, then, would you like to follow me?"

Maggie and Iris followed Mrs Puntz into the post room, a small room adjacent to the office. There was a set of open wooden mailboxes against one wall, and under each was printed the name of a teacher or someone else who worked in the school. Against the other wall was a table, and on it sat a duplicator, a paper cutter, and a large cardboard box filled with rumpled clothing.

"First," said Mrs Puntz, picking up a stack of papers near the duplicator, "I would like you to fold each of these notices in half. Then put one in each cubby hole that has a teacher's name below it. Like this." She demonstrated by slowly and carefully folding one of the notices and putting it in a box.

"Here is Mr Newton's box," said Mrs Puntz. "And the librarian's box, and the cafeteria manager's box, and the janitor's box." She pointed at each one.

Iris yawned loudly, patting her mouth.

"But those boxes don't get notices this time. The notices are only for the classroom teachers." She smiled at the girls. "Okay?"

"Okay," said Maggie.

Iris said nothing.

"After you have done the notice job," continued Mrs Puntz, "you may empty the contents of the lost-and-found box onto the floor and then fold the clothing back into the box. Neatly! Like so." She took a sweater out of the box, flattened it on the table, folded the sleeves behind the front, and then folded the sweater in half.

Maggie pretended to be interested.

Mrs Puntz picked up a handkerchief with a hole in it. "Things like this can be discarded." She walked over and dropped it into the bin. "But you need to ask my permission first before throwing anything out.

"Cheer up," Mrs Puntz said to Iris, patting the top of her head.

But Iris frowned as Mrs Puntz walked out of the room, stepped behind her desk, and sat down – straightening her skirt behind her.

"What a nerd," whispered Iris.

"Shhh!" whispered Maggie. "Here." She picked up a notice from the top of the stack and folded it in half. "I'll fold and you put."

Several of the boxes contained slips of pink memo paper with typewritten messages on them, signed by the principal. Iris pulled one out. "What *is* this!" she said. "How come the guy types everything?"

"Because he's a neat freak," said Maggie. "Don't read!"

Iris tossed the paper back into the box and moved over to Mrs Hall's box. "Get this!" she whispered, tipping her head sideways to read the memo. "He says Mrs Hall should take the extra staples out of the bulletin board in the hall outside our classroom."

"What extra staples?" whispered Maggie.

Iris shrugged. "And get this! He says the bulletin board would have been more attractive if the students had coloured their self-portraits!"

"Our charcoal sketches?" whispered Maggie.

"I guess so. What a jerk!"

Mrs Puntz blew her nose.

"Hurry up!" whispered Maggie. She and Iris quickly distributed notices into the boxes.

Then they walked over to the lost-and-found box. Iris whistled a bombing noise and slid the box from the tabletop. It landed with a thud, upside down, on the floor.

"Brother," said Iris. "Look at this." She pulled a bra out of the wad of tangled clothing and held it in the air by one strap.

Maggie stared at the bra.

"It looks like somebody slept in it for a year. Look at the elastic! Look how yellow it is!"

"Put it back!" said Maggie. She glanced through the doorway at Mrs Puntz.

"It's for a perfectly flat kid," said Iris. "Try it on!"

"Put it back!"

"How are we doing, girls?" called Mrs Puntz.

"Fine," called Maggie. She rummaged through the clothes. She pulled a red cardigan with gum stuck on it out of the box by one sleeve and began buttoning the buttons down the front.

"This bra," whispered Iris. "This bra would fit you perfectly. It's for a totally, *totally* flat kid!"

Maggie rolled her eyes up to meet Iris's. "Will you *shut up?*"

The phone rang in the office.

Iris dangled the bra in front of Maggie's nose.

"I'm ignoring you," said Maggie.

Iris found the label and turned it over. "It's size twenty-eight double A. Perfect! I'll show it to your mother. Didn't you say she wanted me to do some research on bras for flatties? She can modify this for you, Maggie. She can make the cups littler!" She giggled softly.

"Get busy!" Maggie told her. "You're just sitting there! I'm doing all the work!"

"Well, get me the rubbish bin, then."

Maggie pulled the bin over to Iris. "You're supposed to ask Mrs Puntz before you throw anything out."

"Mrs Puntz is on the telephone. It would be rude to interrupt Mrs Puntz when she's on the telephone."

Iris found her empty lunch bag marked IRIS and took it out of the trash.

"What are you doing?" whispered Maggie as Iris rolled up the bra and stuffed it into the paper bag. "Are you crazy?"

Iris jammed the paper bag into her back pocket.

Maggie folded two unmatched dirty socks together and tossed them into the box. She peered through the doorway at Mrs Puntz, who was saying something into the telephone receiver about GIVE A HOOT – DON'T POLLUTE signs. Then she took a sweatshirt with dancing hamburgers on the front out of the box and began folding it. Her mother was right – Iris was nothing but trouble. And face it, if it hadn't been for Iris, Blossom wouldn't have had her stomach carved open like a pumpkin. And what was Iris doing now?

Maggie glared at her.

Iris was standing around with a moth-eaten bra in her pocket – that she'd stolen from the lost-and-found!

The bell rang.

Iris walked over and stood in front of Mrs Puntz's desk.

"Yes, I can understand that, Mr Arnold," said Mrs Puntz into the telephone receiver. "Yes, certainly."

Iris leaned close to Mrs Puntz and mouthed the words "We need a pass." She drew a small square in the air in front of her.

Mrs Puntz covered the mouthpiece with her hand, shook her head at Iris, and made a sour face.

"A pass!" whispered Iris loudly. She pointed to the clock.

Maggie cringed.

"No, no, that won't be necessary, Mr Arnold," said Mrs Puntz into the receiver. Then she said in a sweet voice, "Excuse me, can you hold for a minute?"

Iris tapped the memo pad on Mrs Puntz's desk and pointed to herself. "A pass!"

Mrs Puntz scowled at Iris and held the telephone against her blouse. "Iris! Will you kindly, *kindly* wait until Mr Newton returns? This is someone from the superintendent's office!

"These kids!" said Mrs Puntz cheerily into the telephone. "Now, where were we . . ."

Mr Newton walked in, wearing a maroon polyester suit, a white belt and white shoes, and a lime-green shirt with a plastic pen holder in the pocket. He raised his eyebrows and looked at Mrs Puntz.

She made a yackety-yak motion with her fingers and pointed to the receiver, then closed her eyes and shook her head. She pointed to the memo pad and then to Iris and Maggie.

"Follow me, ladies," said Mr Newton.

They walked into his office.

He ripped a sheet of memo paper from his pad and put it into his typewriter.

"Why do you type everything?" said Iris.

"Neater!" said Mr Newton.

"You were right!" Iris said to Maggie.

Maggie quickly looked away.

TO CLASF typed Mr Newton. "Oops!" he said. He corrected the error carefully with pink correction fluid. TO CLASS – IRIS AND MAGGIE. He looked up at the ceiling for a minute, thinking. Then he typed some more.

Iris rolled her eyes at Maggie and looked at the clock.

Mr Newton ripped the pink paper out of the typewriter, took a pen from the plastic pen holder in his pocket and clicked it once, and wrote GERALD NEWTON on the line at the bottom of the paper. "Off you go!" he said to Iris, handing her the pass.

"My mother calls those plastic pen holders nerd packs," said Iris.

"Nerd packs?" said Mr Newton. "Oh, she does, does she?" He found an empty space for the pen in his pen holder. "Nerd packs," he grumbled quietly. "Well, off you go to class, I said!"

Maggie hurried out of the room, with Iris following her. "What does the note say?" she asked, and Iris read it aloud in her best Mr Newton voice:

" From the desk of Mr Gerald Newton,
principal

To class: Iris and Maggie. I hope these gals have learned their lesson. Remember that

93

Maggie is to return during lunch recesses on Thursday and Friday. Also, *please* see note in your box regarding your bulletin board problems.

Gerald Newton"

"That creep," said Maggie.

"Now you're talking!" said Iris. "I was beginning to think you had turned into a Hilary over this whole thing." She suddenly stopped walking. "Now, what have we here?"

Iris looked closely at the edge of the memo paper "Two memo papers! What *do* you know!"

She separated them.

"So what?" said Maggie.

"So, this one is a blank. A spare!" Iris moved to a window in the hallway and held the paper up to the light. "With a perfect impression of Newt's signature where he pressed so hard. See? Gerald Newton."

"Let's go," said Maggie.

Iris kissed the paper. "I could type whatever I wanted to on this paper, do you realize that? And trace Mr Newton's signature!"

Maggie looked at Iris with a serious expression. "But that would be forgery, Iris. Have you lost your mind?"

"Yes," said Iris. "Forgery it would be. And think of the possibilities! Think!" said Iris, tapping her finger on the side of her head and staring at Maggie with a crazed look in her eyes. "Think of the possibilities for Corky retaliation!"

Maggie watched without speaking as Iris carefully slid the memo paper into her back pocket.

Think of the possibilities! Maggie couldn't think of any possibilities – all she could think of was that she was beginning to wish she'd never met Iris.

"Listen," she said. She turned and put her hand on Iris's shoulder. "I mean this: I don't want to have anything to do with you forging anything on that pink paper in your back pocket. Or that bra you ripped off from the lost and found!"

Iris smiled at Maggie.

"I mean it, Iris. It's not funny."

"It is too."

"No, it isn't. It's serious!"

"Lighten up," said Iris. She started to walk away.

Maggie caught up to her. "Iris, I really, seriously mean that I don't want you to show that bra to my mother. I don't even want a bra! Look, I have enough trouble at home. And Iris –"

Iris turned to Maggie.

"My mother doesn't want me to be friends with you any more."

Iris stopped walking. "Are you serious? Not ever?"

"I don't think so. Neither does my father. It's the only thing they agree on."

Iris searched Maggie's eyes. "Well, what about you? Do you want to be friends with me? Or do your parents make all your decisions for you?"

Maggie didn't answer.

They walked slowly toward the classroom door.

"There you are!" said Mrs Hall. "I almost sent a search party out after you. Do you have a pass?"

Iris handed her the note from Mr Newton.

Mrs Hall read the note and then gazed out of the doorway at the bulletin board, a thoughtful expression on her face. Then with one finger she pushed her glasses farther up on the bridge of her nose and said, "Where were we?"

Iris and Maggie walked down the aisle to their desks. "Iris," whispered Corky as she walked by, "what's in the bag? Hair sandwiches for your friend?"

"Shut up," said Iris. She opened her desktop and tossed the bag inside. "It's none of your business."

"I can make it my business," whispered Corky. "I'm clean-up captain, remember?"

# 13

"I suppose i should shove those boxes into the garage," said Maggie's mother. "They'll only get heavier if they get wet."

"I'll do that," said Maggie. She picked up her empty plate and glass, cleared them from the dinner table, and ran outside.

The boxes were already spotted with rain; she slid them into the garage.

A white ceramic lamp without a shade poked out of the top of one of the boxes. Maggie pulled it out by the cord. There were pictures of elephants painted on the base with blue glaze – each was holding another's tail in its trunk.

She wondered why her mother would throw away such a good lamp. She stood it on the workbench next to a socket, plugged it in, and pulled the beaded chain.

It even worked!

And in the light of the elephant lamp, Maggie began poking around in the other boxes she'd brought in from the rain.

In one there was a stack of white bloomer athletic shorts and a faded sweatshirt with a cracked rubber dove on the front that had PEACE written on its wings.

She took out a pair of the shorts and, stretching the elastic waistband with her thumbs, held the shorts against her. *These are great*, she thought. But when she read HARVARD on one leg, she put them back into the box. It didn't seem like a very good idea to wear shorts that said HARVARD on them at this point – although it was a shame to throw away perfectly good white balloony shorts like Iris's.

Underneath the stack of clothes, Maggie found a grey paper folder. It was spotted with mildew and smelled like mushrooms. Maggie took it out and opened it up.

Inside was a picture of her father, wearing shorts and a red T-shirt with white piping on the sleeves and an *H* on the front. He was holding a racket. Was it a squash racket?

Maggie stared at the photograph. Her father's hair was thick and curly – and long! He was smiling.

It was true, what people said. She slowly ran her tongue across her teeth. She did look like her father.

Maggie read what he had written on the bottom of the picture:

> Rosie–
>
> *"All the stars are a-bloom with flowers . . ."*
>
> > Yours till the last,
> >
> > Dave

When was the last time her father had called her mother Rosie?

Maggie couldn't remember.

When was the last time her mother had called her father Dave?

"What's that?" asked Dinah, walking into the garage.

"A picture." Maggie closed the folder.

"Of what?"

"Of Dad." Maggie opened the folder under Dinah's nose and slapped it closed again. She tossed it into the box. "Does Mum know you're out here? You haven't even got a jumper on." Maggie ushered Dinah out of the door.

Dinah raced ahead.

But Maggie walked more slowly toward the house, wondering why a picture of her father would be in the garage in a box marked DUMP.

Should she really leave a picture of her father in a box marked DUMP?

Maggie turned round. The window was lit. The lamp was still on.

She hurried back and ducked under the door.

She turned off the light and stood there for a moment, listening to the rain. It was falling more heavily now; the roof was rattling.

A gust of wind blew a garden chair over outside the door.

Maggie buttoned up her cardigan. She stood in the doorway and looked out across the yard at her house. The kitchen window was a yellow square; she could see her mother moving behind the curtains.

Maggie quickly took the photograph of her father out of the cardboard box and pushed it up inside her sweater. *Now I actually do qualify as perfectly flat*, she thought.

She picked out the pair of Harvard shorts, rolled them up, and stuffed them under the front of her sweater.

*Better*, she told herself.

And she hurried back across the soggy lawn and into the house.

Whistling quietly, she went into her bedroom and shut the door. She slid the portrait of her father out from underneath her cardigan and put it, along with the shorts, in the bottom of her underwear drawer.

She lay down on her bed and crossed her legs at the ankles. She felt pooped, but she still had to work on her family portrait poem. Her mother poked her head round the door. "Tired?"

"A little," said Maggie. She sat up on the edge of her bed and rubbed her eyes.

Her mother sat beside her. "It's been a long day. But I'm making headway out there. I can even see my old potter's kick wheel through the clutter."

Maggie slowly blinked.

"Mum? Did you mean to throw away all that stuff in those boxes?"

Her mother nodded.

"All of it? Even the lamp with elephants on it? It still works!"

"Close your eyes," whispered her mother. "Listen to the rain."

Maggie tipped her head onto her mother's shoulder.

She woke up the next morning with all her clothes on, except her shoes.

Maggie washed and changed. She felt a little guilty as she opened her underwear drawer, so she put on a vest.

At breakfast she asked her mother if Hilary could come to play one day soon, and her mother said yes.

On her way to school Maggie told her mother she'd changed her mind about the bra. She didn't need a bra – at least not yet – and her mother agreed.

They arrived at school fifteen minutes early; Maggie was determined to work on her family portrait poem. She waved good-bye to her mother and hurried across the yard.

Iris jumped out from behind the outside stairwell. *"Ha!"* she said in Maggie's face. "Smell my breath!"

"Spaghetti?" said Maggie.

"No, pizza," said Iris. "I had pizza for breakfast. And I brought pizza for my snack."

Iris motioned for Maggie to come back behind the stairwell.

"I have to finish my family portrait poem," said Maggie.

"Quick!" said Iris.

Maggie walked behind the stairwell.

Iris looked first in one direction, then the other. Then she showed Maggie a large clasp envelope that had been wrapped in a sweater. Fastened to the top edge with a paper clip was a small piece of pink memo paper with FROM THE DESK OF MR GERALD NEWTON, PRINCIPAL printed on it. "Recognize this?" said Iris. "Read it!"

There was a typewritten message on it that said:

MRS HALL:

YOUR CLEAN-UP CAPTAIN, CORKY NEWTON, HAS FOUND AND TURNED IN TO THE OFFICE YOUR BRASSIERE. KINDLY DO NOT LEAVE YOUR UNDERGARMENTS STREWN ABOUT IN THE HALL-WAY OUTSIDE YOUR CLASSROOM. IT SETS A

And on the line at the bottom for a signature Iris had
carefully traced the imprint of the principal's name in
ballpoint pen.

"Iris!" whispered Maggie.

"The bra's inside," said Iris. She rapidly raised and
lowered her eyebrows. "And I'm going to put it in Mrs
Hall's mailbox!"

Maggie stared at Iris.

"Don't you get it?" whispered Iris. "Mrs Hall will
get this envelope with the bra and the note in it, and
she'll think that Corky Newton thought the bra was
hers and turned it in to the office. She'll think Corky
told Mr Newton this bra was *hers*!" she giggled. "Don't
you get it?"

"I get it," said Maggie, turning away.

She walked out and began to climb the stairs.

"Wait!" cried Iris.

"You're on your own with that trick," said Maggie
in a low voice. "Just don't get me involved."

"I won't!" said Iris. "Relax." She stopped Maggie by
putting her hand on Maggie's shoulder. "Look, this is
between me and Corky Newton. There's a score that
needs settling, that's all. And it doesn't involve you,
okay?"

Maggie moved Iris's hand off her shoulder and
continued up the steps without speaking.

Iris ran ahead of her and waited at the top. "Why are
you so opposed to giving Corky Newton a little grief?"

Maggie looked at Iris. "You mean giving Mrs Hall a
little grief, don't you?"

"Oh, come *on*. Mrs Hall's a grown woman. What

does she care? She'll probably just hold the bra up in front of the class and ask Corky Newton why he would think such a tiny little bra would fit her. You know how huge her–"

"Shhh!" whispered Maggie.

"Well, you know they couldn't possibly fit–"

"Okay!" whispered Maggie.

"Well? You're not interested in embarrassing Corky Newton?"

Maggie didn't answer. But yes, she was interested in embarrassing Corky Newton. She was interested in doing a lot more than that to Corky Newton.

"Move," she said to Iris.

Iris blocked her path. "Admit it. It's a good trick."

"I'm not admitting anything," said Maggie. But in her heart she did think it was a good trick.

"Then at least admit that it's funny."

Maggie softly bit the insides of her cheeks to keep from smiling.

"See?" said Iris. "You think it's funny."

"I said move," said Maggie. "I'm not even supposed to be talking to you."

They giggled as they walked through the doorway and down the hall.

Outside the principal's office Hilary waved and walked over to Maggie.

"Mrs Puntz!" Iris called into the office. "Mrs Puntz! I can't find my catcher's mitt! I need to check the lost and found!"

"What catcher's mitt?" said Hilary to Maggie, and Maggie shrugged. They peered into the doorway.

"My sainted aunt," said Mrs Puntz. "What would you be doing with a catcher's mitt?" She was measuring some ground coffee in a plastic cup to put in the electric coffee machine. "Why, when I was a girl you wouldn't have caught me dead playing baseball. I had s'dern much fun with my little red play iron. Course, it didn't plug in, but what did I care! I was just as happy as a little clam, pressing my doll's gowns and things . . ."

Iris wasn't listening. She had barged into the mail room and stuffed the clasp envelope into Mrs Hall's mailbox. Then she pretended to look through the lost and found.

"It isn't in there," she announced to Mrs Puntz.

"No," continued Mrs Puntz, "I wouldn't have dreamed of playing baseball when I was a child!" She poured a beaker of water into the electric coffeepot.

"Well, maybe that's why you stand around making pots of coffee for Mr Newton instead of making a million dollars a year playing for the Yankees," called Iris.

She hurried out of the office.

Maggie was yakking with Hilary just outside. She covered her ears. "I don't want to know, don't tell me anything about it, la la la la la la, I'm not listening to you!" she said to Iris.

Iris threw up her arms.

They walked to their classroom and sat down just as the bell was ringing.

Mrs Hall was standing at the front of the class, itching the top of her head with a pencil. Her registration book was in her hand.

She surveyed the class, frowning at a few stragglers who came rushing in, then wrote *A* for absent in front of Corky Newton's name and shut the book.

"Hilary," she said, "would you take the registration book to the office? Also, check my pigeonhole just after break will you? I have yard duty today."

Hilary nodded. She left the room with the registration book.

Mrs Hall had written the daily schedule on the board: writing family portrait poems, reading, break, spelling, lunch, poetry recital, science, break, social studies.

Iris looked over at Maggie. "He's absent," she whispered. "Rats!"

Maggie took out her family portrait poem and decided absolutely to never have anything more to do with Iris. Ever. Theft, forgery, tampering with the mail – this was getting out of hand.

Maggie thought up the last couple of lines for her poem and wrote them down.

Then she crossed out the line she'd written about Iris.

Finished. And finished with Iris.

She put the poem away, took out *The Ella Fitzgerald Story*, and began to read.

But she couldn't concentrate.

"I'm going to the library," she said to Iris when the break bell rang. "Don't follow me."

Maggie walked into the library and sat down. She opened *The Ella Fitzgerald Story* and began reading it. But as she was reading, her mind kept wandering – to Iris. And Corky Newton, that rat. Where was he, anyway?

Iris was going to get into trouble. You weren't supposed to put things in teachers' pigeonholes – especially old bras. And especially with notes on them, forged with the principal's signature.

Maggie put the book in her lap.

Mrs Hall was a nice teacher. Hadn't she even offered Maggie half of her sandwich? So what if Maggie hated paté. That wasn't the point.

She was a nice teacher with a sense of humour.

Sort of.

Maggie stood up and strolled to the windows.

Outside, girls were walking arm in arm, skipping, drawing hopscotch squares on the ground with chalk.

She looked for Iris and saw her, slamming the tetherball around the pole while a group of boys looked on.

Maggie turned from the window and quietly crossed the carpet. She picked up one of the rocks the librarian had put out for display.

Mrs Williams walked up to her and smiled. "How's that doggy?"

Maggie turned round. "She's fine."

"And how are you?"

"Oh, I don't know," said Maggie. She put the rock back on the shelf.

"Two days in a row in the library at break!" said Mrs Williams. "Is this a trend?"

Maggie sighed. "To tell you the truth, I'm avoiding Iris."

"Well, that might not be a bad idea. What is it this time?"

"The usual," said Maggie. "But this time I think she's really about to get herself in trouble."

"Well," said Mrs Williams, "what can you do? As long as you're not involved, it's Iris's problem. Right? As long as you're not a co-conspirator!"

"Right," said Maggie.

And Mrs Williams was right. As long as she wasn't involved, it was Iris's problem. As long as she wasn't a co-conspirator.

What was a co-conspirator?

"Mrs Williams," she said suddenly. "Could I use

your telephone? It's an emergency! I need to talk to my dad!"

But what Maggie had almost said was "I need to talk to a lawyer."

"Of course, Maggie," said the librarian. "If it's an emergency. But you need to press nine first. And wait for the dial tone."

Maggie rushed into the office.

"Law offices," said the receptionist who answered. "May I help you?"

"This is Maggie. May I please talk to my dad?"

"Mr Hunter? I'm sorry. He's stepped out to meet a client. Can I get him to return your call?"

"I'm at school," said Maggie. She paused. "Is Samantha there?"

"Well, she's in a meeting right now. Is this urgent?"

Maggie thought for a moment. Was this urgent?

"Yes."

"If you'll hold a minute. I'll see if I can interrupt her," said the receptionist. The phone clicked, and some symphony music began to play in Maggie's ear.

She listened and waited.

She watched the second hand sweep round the clock.

The break bell rang.

Maggie listened to violins and cellos and watched the other students gather their belongings and leave the library.

She couldn't wait any longer, so she hung up the phone. She waved good-bye to Mrs Williams and quickly went back to her classroom and sat down.

A few seconds later Hilary huffed into the room, with Iris following her. She put a couple of printed bulletins and a small white envelope on top of

107

Mrs Hall's desk, and then the large and puffy clasp envelope she had been clutching to her chest.

"Thank you," said Mrs Hall.

Mrs Hall skimmed the two bulletins, then opened and read the note that was in the small envelope.

She squeezed the large envelope as she read the message typed on the memo stapled to the front. She frowned. Then she glanced up at the class with her lips pressed together so that her mouth looked quite thin and sour.

Mrs Hall sat down in her chair behind her desk and, putting the envelope in her lap, opened the clasp and pulled the bra out part of the way. She gasped and covered her mouth with her hand.

She shoved the bra back into the envelope and stood up. Then she ripped the pink note from the envelope screwed it up in one hand, and marched over to the litter bin and threw it in. She raised her skirt and lifted her leg to stomp the rubbish further down into the bottom of the bin.

Iris looked up from her spelling workbook and scratched the side of her neck. She looked slyly over at Maggie, who was holding her workbook in front of her nose.

Maggie peeked over the top of the book. Mrs Hall had walked back to her desk, opened the drawer, and slapped one of her FROM THE DESK OF MARY HALL notepads on her desktop. She scribbled a message, emphatically dotting her *i's* and crossing her *t's*, and then tore it from the memo pad.

Maggie's heart fluttered.

Mrs Hall sighed heavily several times. Then, biting the corner of her bottom lip, she wrote another, shorter message. She jerked out a long piece of sticky tape from the metal tape dispenser and, holding the note she had written against the clasp envelope, plastered tape across the note. Then she jerked out more tape and slapped and whacked each piece into place.

She shoved the envelope to one corner of her desk and drummed her fingers on her desktop, occasionally raising and lowering one eyebrow. Then she stood up, ripped the message and the tape from the envelope, wadded it up, and went to the litter bin. She frantically shook her hand over the can because the message was stuck to her fingers.

Mrs Hall grabbed the stapler from her desk and flipped it open. She walked out to the bulletin board and began slamming staples randomly into the surface.

"What's with her?" somebody asked.

But nobody answered – least of all Maggie, who had gone numb. She just sat there, looking at her fingers. They no longer felt as though they were attached to her hands, which seemed like somebody else's hands folded in front of her. *Calm down*, she tried to tell herself. *This is not your problem*. But she couldn't calm down.

Mrs Hall stormed back into the room. "Who wants to make some more black and white charcoal drawings to put on the bulletin board instead of doing spelling? Well, don't just sit there, then! Joel? Stella? Pass out the paper. And no crayons! No crayons, paint, or coloured chalk. Understand? No colour!"

# 14

MAGGIE WALKED DOWN the hallway alone. Her stomach felt empty – and uneasy. She went into the office and sat down.

She opened her lunch. Inside was a yogurt drink from Mrs Wiggle's Rocket Juice Company. She undid the purple cap and drank the yogurt. She replaced the cap and took a plastic bag full of trail mix out of the paper bag. She ate it, avoiding the squares of dried papaya.

Mrs Puntz looked up at Maggie. "You're a very well-behaved little girl without your sidekick," she said.

Maggie tried to smile.

Mrs Hall walked in briskly, clutching the clasp envelope. She went right past Mrs Puntz to Mr Newton's doorway. "Where is he?" she asked in a serious voice.

Maggie's heart raced.

"He's with the caretaker," said Mrs Puntz. "Somebody dropped pizza on the playground at snack time and one of Mrs Collins's little ones stepped in it and then trailed it all over the school."

Mrs Hall took a wide-tipped red marker from a circular container on Mrs Puntz's desk. "May I?"

But before Mrs Puntz could answer, Mrs Hall had

110

begun to scrawl a message across the front of the envelope – so big that Maggie could easily read it from across the room:

DOES THIS LOOK LIKE IT WOULD FIT ME?

Mrs Hall tossed the envelope onto Mrs Puntz's blotter and practically threw the marker back into the container. Then she whacked her palms together as if she were clapping dust from her hands and stood with her fists on her hips. "Give that to him the minute he returns."

"Yes, of course," said Mrs Puntz, looking quite alarmed.

Mrs Hall turned to leave the room. "Maggie!" she said. "I didn't see you sitting there! You look as though you've seen a ghost! Are you all right?"

"Yes," squeaked Maggie. "Yes," she said again, in her regular voice. "Yes, I'm fine."

Mrs Hall left the office.

Mrs Puntz looked at Maggie and pretended to smile. "Everyone ready to be a junior secretary should follow me!"

Maggie followed her into the workroom. She wasn't really ready to be a junior secretary, though; she was ready to go home.

"One. Two. Three. Staple!" said Mrs Puntz as she demonstrated to Maggie how to pick up papers from the table in order and where to staple them. "Then make a stack of them here. Like so."

Maggie picked up one paper from the top of each of the three piles and stapled them together at the corner.

"Good," said Mrs Puntz. "Now staple up a storm!" She left Maggie and returned to her desk.

A few minutes later Maggie heard Mr Newton come into the office. "Hello, hello," he said to Mrs Puntz. He stood in front of her desk for a moment, shaking his head.

A piece of pizza was stuck to his shoe.

"What a mess out there," he said. "But thanks to me, and the caretaker, it's under control."

Mrs Puntz smiled.

"Who would send their child to school with a pizza for a snack?" said Mr Newton. "Put a note in next week's parent bulletin instructing parents *please* not to send pizza or other messy foods to school for snack or lunch, would you?"

"Surely," said Mrs Puntz.

Mr Newton winked. "You're a doll! And would you make a fresh pot of coffee? I deserve a fresh cup of coffee after that fiasco!"

"Yes, and here!" said Mrs Puntz, handing him the clasp envelope. "Mrs Hall asked me to give this to you. She seemed – excited when she dropped it by. And anxious for you to have it right away."

Mr Newton walked into the office with the envelope, leaving small tracks of tomato sauce on the rug.

Maggie's heart was pounding behind her ribs. *Take it easy*, she told herself. *You have nothing to do with this!*

She stapled three more groups of three papers and heard Mr Newton say in a quiet voice, "Mrs Puntz, would you step into my office for a minute?"

Mrs Puntz got up from the chair and went to Mr Newton's office doorway.

"May I ask you a question?" said Mr Newton. "I need your opinion – as a woman."

"Yes? . . ."

"What size brassière do you think Mrs Hall would wear?"

Mrs Puntz frowned at Mr Newton. "Brassière?" She stared at him. "Why, Mr Newton," she said sharply, "I don't have any idea what size brassière Mrs Hall would wear. Why would you ask?"

Mr Newton stood up behind his desk. "Well, put it this way," he said. He held up the bra and let it dangle in the air in front of him. "Do you think this would fit her?"

"I wouldn't know!" said Mrs Puntz. She whirled around, and in a huff, marched back to her desk and sat down. "What size brassière would Mrs Hall wear – indeed!" she grumbled.

Mr Newton walked out of his office.

Maggie could see the elastic and hooks of the bra hanging out of his jacket pocket.

"You don't understand –" he said.

Mrs Puntz glared at him with one eyebrow cocked.

"Mrs Hall asked my opinion on whether or not this brassière would fit her." He pulled his jacket pocket open and looked hard at the bra. "And quite frankly, I think it would be too small."

"Oh, you do, do you!" said Mrs Puntz in an icy voice. "How perceptive you are, Mr Newton! But why would Mrs Hall need to ask you what size brassière she wears?" She cleared her throat. She unsnapped her glasses case, put on her glasses, and pretended to read something typed on a piece of paper. "I hardly think" she continued, "that I want to be involved in a guessing game between you and Mrs Hall about the size of her" – she paused – "brassière!" She glared at Mr Newton.

"Calm down," he told her.

"Calm down, nothing!" cried Mrs Puntz. "And let me add this: I have no intention of making you coffee while you sit in your office noodling about women's undergarments. So make your own darn coffee from now on. Why should I make your coffee? I could be a baseball player, for Lord's sake, making a million dollars a year!

"Good heavens!" she cried. "I forgot you were here!" she said to Maggie, who had moved to the doorway when the bell rang. "Run along, now, you're excused. And never mind the pass!"

Maggie walked quickly to her classroom and sat down, quite out of breath.

She opened her desktop and ducked behind it. She looked at Iris, then closed her eyes and shook her head.

"Family portrait poems," said Mrs Hall. "Who's ready?" She picked up her mark book.

Iris raised her hand.

"Iris?"

Iris walked to the front of the room and slowly opened a piece of paper that was folded into a small square. "This poem is about my grandmother.

> "I've seen Gram naked.
> She's got bigger buns
> than anyone's.
> When she showers
> she wears a rubber bathing cap
> with rubber flowers.
> I shout at her!
> But she never hears—
> unless she puts the flaps up
> with the snaps up
> past her ears."

Mrs Hall sighed. "Is that it?"

Iris nodded.

Mrs Hall chewed on the end of her pencil for a moment, then wrote a little B- next to Iris's name in her mark book.

"A boy next. Who's ready?" She looked up. "William?"

William pointed to his chest. "Me?"

"Is your name William?"

"Yes."

"Would you like to come up here and read your family portrait poem?"

"My dog ate my paper," lied William.

"Why would a dog eat your paper, William?"

"I don't know," said William. "I have a pen that smells like chili."

The door opened, and Corky Newton strutted into the room, wearing new trousers, new white leather high-tops and a new shirt with football numbers on it. "My mum took me clothes shopping," he announced loudly, turning to the class and making a muscleman pose. "The Guess jeans are compliments of Maggie's father."

"Clothes shopping?" said Mrs Hall coolly. "On a school day? That seems rather inappropriate. Did your uncle, the principal, accept that as a legal excuse to be late?"

Corky's neck got red. "Yes."

"Oh, he did," said Mrs Hall. She began to walk slowly back and forth in front of the blackboard. "Tell us, Corky, how was the shopping expedition?"

"Fine," said Corky. He looked at the floor and headed to his seat.

"Oh, don't sit down!" said Mrs Hall. "We want to

115

know – did you happen to see any undergarments lying around the store?"

"No!" said Corky.

Somebody laughed.

"Well, how about outside the store?"

"No!" cried Corky. "Why?"

"Just wondering," said Mrs Hall. "You seem to be the champ when it comes to spotting underwear."

"Thank you," said Corky. He glanced at Iris, and she tried to block a giggle but it snorted through her nose. "Because underwear is the subject of my clean-up captain's morning report."

Hilary turned to Maggie and whispered. "Now he wants to look in people's underwear?"

"And," continued Corky, "*since* I was absent this morning, I would like to give it now."

"Well, you may *not* give it now," said Mrs Hall. "Get your family portrait poem."

Corky quickly walked to his desk and then back up to the front of the room. "My family portrait poyme," he read in a loud voice. He looked at the class and smiled.

Maggie smiled at him, her elbow on her desk and her fist against her cheek.

"What's a poyme?" whispered Iris.

"Go ahead," said Mrs Hall to Corky. "We're listening."

"I'd like to wait until Maggie and Iris quit making faces at each other."

Mrs Hall looked at Maggie and Iris. Both of them were watching Corky with the same bored expression.

"Go ahead, please."

"My family portrait poyme," said Corky. He took a deep breath and read:

"Roses are red,
violets are blue.
I have a family
just like you.
We live in a house
with a picket fence.
My favourite candy
is peppermints."

"Pepper*mints*," said Mrs Hall. She looked down at
her book and wrote a tiny C- near Corky's name. "And
speaking of pepper*mints*," she said. "It was brought to
my attention this morning by someone in this classroom that you have been opening desks and snooping
in them, saying it is your job as clean-up captain to do
so. And then asking for things in desks – like
pepper*mints*."

Corky opened his mouth and drew in a deep breath.
"Who said that?"

"Have you?"

"No! Honest to God!"

Hilary gasped. "You have too, you liar!"

"I have not!" said Corky. "Not to snoop, I haven't.
To check for ants, yes. But not to snoop. Of course, if I
happen to see something unusual . . .or if someone
decides to give me a small gift for my services . . ."

"Listen," said Mrs Hall. "Let me make something
clear to you. I'm getting a little fed up with this clean-
up captain business, especially after an incident that
happened involving an article of clothing that you
found and turned in to the office yesterday and you
know exactly what I'm talking about *and* I will discuss
that *and a few other things with you at break!*"

117

"But–"

Sit down!"

Looking wounded, Corky walked back to his seat. On his way past Hilary's desk, he walked over the toe of her shoe.

"Ouch!"

"Sorry!" said Corky. "Sorry – really!" He turned to Mrs Hall. "It was an accident," he told her, and sat down.

There was a knock at the door.

"Come in," said Mrs Hall.

Mr Newton stuck his head into the room and smiled. "May I speak to you for a moment?"

Mrs Hall stared at him, her eyes blazing. "Yes, you may!" She slapped her mark book closed and threw it onto her desk, then straightened the lapel of her suit jacket and walked briskly out of the room, slamming the door behind her.

The room grew quiet.

Maggie heard Mr Newton talking, but she couldn't hear what he said. Whatever he was saying, she decided, was going to mean trouble for Iris.

She looked over at Iris.

Iris looked different, as if she'd grown taller, or older, or something. Or maybe she looked just a little too big for her chair. Her legs were fully extended; they were much too long to be comfortable any other way.

She was looking in the direction of the door. Her jaw was set, her head was high. Her arms were crossed on her chest.

Suddenly the class heard Mrs Hall shriek, "What do you *mean* you think my breasts are entirely too large for my brassière?"

Maggie heard a loud slap outside the door. Then she heard footsteps rushing away.

The door handle turned, and Mrs Hall walked in. "Now where were we?" she said in a spirited voice.

Nobody spoke.

"Why are you all staring at me? Who's next with family portrait poems?" she asked cheerily. She surveyed the room. "Maggie! You've gone pale again! Are you all right?"

Maggie nodded, but she wasn't so sure she was all right.

"Then come on up and read your poem!"

Maggie walked to the front of the room with her spiral notebook. She opened it to the page where the poem was written and held it in front of her face so she wouldn't have to look at the kids. Maggie read:

" There are flowers growing close to me.
A dog, Blossom. And a Rose."

She paused. And skipped the next three lines.

~~And Iris~~
~~who's almost~~
~~in my family.~~
"My dad was once a champ at squash –
which is something Rose
now grows.
And I suppose–
at the end
I should mention Dinah
(who I wish would take a trip to China
And bring her imaginary friend)."

"A squash isn't a kind of flower!" shouted Corky, throwing up his hands and shaking his head. "It's a vegetable!"

Mrs Hall said nothing. She wrote an A- to Maggie's name. Then she made a small cross in the behaviour column near Corky's name. "One more outburst like that, Captain Underwear, and you'll be washing blackboards after school!"

"Me!" said Corky. "Why shouldn't Iris? She's the one always shooting off her mouth, and you never say anything to her! Besides, *she's* the one you should be asking about underwear – not *me!*" He looked at Iris to make sure she was listening. "She's the one who had a brassière in her desk – that she *stole* from the lost-and-found box –"

"Why don't you shut up, Corky?" said Iris. "And what were you doing, looking in my desk?"

"I saw it there! I saw it in an old lunch bag – that I thought might be attracting insects. And that same brassière, that same one, was in the lost-and-found box in the office. It was!" he cried, turning to Mrs Hall. "I saw it there when I was looking for spare trousers to wear, after I sat in the cheese. Isn't that stealing, Mrs Hall? Isn't it?"

Mrs Hall closed her eyes and put her hand on her forehead.

"Isn't it?" said Corky again.

Mrs Hall didn't answer. She just slowly opened her eyes and stared at Iris.

Iris smiled and waved her fingers just a little bit at Mrs Hall and said in a small voice, "It was only a joke."

Mrs Hall said nothing. She just stood there, staring at Iris, her eyes like hard-boiled eggs.

"See?" said Corky. He looked around the room at

the other students. "It *is* stealing!"

"Sit down, Corky," said Mrs Hall without taking her eyes off Iris. "And put your head down. All of you, put your heads down on your desks. Iris, you come with me."

Maggie rested her face on her arms and peeked out above her elbow at Iris.

"What about Maggie?" said Corky from the back of the room.

Maggie lifted her head.

Iris looked over at her. "Put your head down!"

"What about Maggie?" said Corky again, from the back of the room. "She was with Iris in the office, wasn't she? Didn't she have to help fold the things in the lost-and-found?"

"Why don't you stay out of this!" cried Iris.

Maggie didn't move.

Mrs Hall looked at Maggie for a long time. "Are you part of this, Maggie? Were you with Iris when she took the brassière from the lost-and-found?"

"No!" cried Iris.

"I'm talking to Maggie. Maggie, did you know that Iris took the brassière from the lost-and-found?"

"Yes, but –"

"Did you know Iris put it in my mailbox? Did you know she forged Mr Newton's signature?"

Maggie looked at the floor. "Yes."

"You knew that Iris had put the brassière in the envelope, and you didn't tell me when you saw me bring it into the office? You just sat there and let me do that? Maggie!" cried Mrs Hall. "What's come over you!"

# 15

"Suspended from school!" said Maggie's mother as they walked down the school steps.

Maggie was blinking back tears.

They walked together along the pavement towards the car. "I had to pay a baby-sitter so that I could sit in the principal's office and listen to a lecture about undergarments and the honour system!"

"Sorry," said Maggie.

"And what I don't understand is how you managed to get tangled up in another one of Iris's schemes! Or why! Or was this another one of your father's brilliant ideas, putting brassières in mailboxes – like putting pigs in dormitory rooms!"

"No! It was Iris's idea!"

"Forge the principal's signature to make a fool of his nephew? What an ingenious plan! But tell me something: Doesn't Iris know that there are consequences to her acts? Doesn't she care that Mrs Hall could have lost her job for smacking the principal across the face?"

"Iris didn't know that Mrs Hall would smack the principal," said Maggie. "How could she know something like that? It was just a joke – that backfired."

"Well, you can say that again – with both of you booted out of the school for two days. And I'm wondering: Why did you girls steal the bra in the first place?" She threw up her arms. "Why?"

"It was just an old bra that didn't belong to anybody."

"Everything belongs to somebody!" cried Maggie's mother. "Everything!"

"Okay," said Maggie.

"The point is that you and Iris took something that didn't belong to you. And that's stealing!"

"Iris took it."

"You were with her."

"But I told her not to!"

Maggie's mother fumbled in her pocket for the keys. "Don't tell me. What's *he* doing here?"

Maggie's father had pulled up beside them in his Mercedes. He opened the window on the passenger side and leaned across the front seat. "What's going on?"

"Dad!" cried Maggie. "What are you doing here?"

"What's happening? Samantha said my receptionist said you hung up before she could take your call."

Maggie's mother turned to Maggie. "You called Samantha? Why would you call Samantha?"

"I called Dad's office," said Maggie. "I needed to talk to a lawyer."

"About what?"

Her father got out of the car. "Would someone kindly tell me what's going on?"

"Your daughter's been suspended from school," called Maggie's mother. "That's what's going on. And isn't this a great time for you to show up – after the fact! I've been sitting in the principal's office being lectured on the topic of brassières!"

Maggie's father looked at Maggie.

"Get in the car," said Maggie's mother, opening the door for Maggie. She glared at Maggie's father. "You're blocking me. You're parked in the middle of the road! Do you want to finish up the week by causing an accident in the middle of the street outside the school?"

"Calm down, Rose." A Volkswagen pulled up behind his car and beeped. "The cars can go round me."

He leaned down and looked at Maggie. "I want to know what happened."

"Iris took a bra from the lost-and-found," she told him.

"Stole a bra," said her mother.

"And she put it in Mrs Hall's box in the teacher's post room – to get back at Corky Newton," said Maggie.

"An extension to your original idea, no doubt," said her mother.

"A note was on it. It said it was from Mr Newton," said Maggie. "But it wasn't."

"Now you've lost me," said Maggie's father.

"The kid forged his name!" cried Maggie's mother. "Can you believe it?"

"So Mrs Hall got mad and slapped him," said Maggie. "I knew about it, but I didn't tell. I didn't know what to do! I tried to call you from the library!"

"I know, I wasn't there. I'm sorry."

"Because," said Maggie's mother, "let me guess." She began to swing her key ring on the end of her finger. "You weren't there because you were at a piano bar, having a three-martini lunch."

Maggie's father stood up. "Get off it, Rose! Will you give me a break!"

124

Maggie's mother lifted an eyebrow. "Give *you* a break? Haven't you had all the breaks there are to have?"

Maggie quickly got into the car and slumped down in the seat.

"When do I get a break?" said Maggie's mother.

The keys flew off the end of her finger, and Maggie's father stepped on them as she leaned down to pick them up. "What do you want from me, Rose?"

"I want you to move your shoe," she told him. "Before I break every toe on your foot."

He kicked the keys sideways into the grass and picked them up. And tossed and caught them.

"I just want you to tell me: When's the war over?" he said. "When's the war over, Rose?"

She didn't answer. She just held out her hand until he dropped the keys into it.

She got into the car and slammed the door.

And when he approached the window to say something else, Maggie's mother rolled it closed. She pumped the accelerator and started the engine, then drummed her fingers on the steering wheel until he gave up and drove away.

She looked over at Maggie.

Maggie fiddled with the drawstring on the pack in her lap.

Her mother pulled away from the kerb. "You didn't think of calling me, did you?" she said in a quiet voice.

Maggie didn't answer.

They drove past the park. Maggie saw a man wearing mirrored sunglasses sitting on a bench with a dog in his lap. She saw kids swinging on aluminium horses, kids going round and round on a circular piece

125

of playground equipment. She saw a mother catch her baby at the bottom of the slide.

"Life used to be so simple," said Maggie.

"What's that supposed to mean?"

Maggie watched a father watching his baby girl try to push an umbrella stroller across the grass.

"She'll never make it," whispered Maggie.

"What?"

"The little girl – she'll never make it. It's too hard. And it's too bumpy. The wheels are getting stuck."

"Quit changing the subject."

"I'm not."

"Then tell me, why did you call your father and not me? Did you forget your own telephone number?"

"No," said Maggie. "I didn't forget my telephone – numbers."

"Well, why didn't you call and ask me for advice? I was home. I would have been happy to give you my opinion. And I would have been happy to give you my opinion of stealing from the lost-and-found."

"I didn't steal anything! Why is it stealing to take something somebody was just going to throw away?"

"I told you! It didn't belong to you!"

Maggie's chest felt so tight that it was hard to fill her lungs with air.

She yawned to catch her breath.

"Tired?" said her mother. "Well, so am I." She pulled into the driveway and jerked up the hand brake. "I'm tired of everything." She turned off the engine.

"Mum?"

"What?"

"Nothing."

"What!"

"I was wondering – why did I get suspended just because I knew?"

"Oh, let's not go through this, Maggie." Her mother pulled on the door handle and the door swung open. She stared blankly at the gravel in the driveway. "You heard the principal – it's the honour system. You were supposed to tell on Iris."

"Tell on my best friend?"

Her mother got out of the car, walked into the garage, and sat on a cardboard box with her elbow on her knee and her fist against her cheek.

Maggie followed her. "I'm supposed to tell on my best friend? What does that have to do with honour?" She walked up to her mother. "And Mum! What does Mr Newton know about honour?"

"Who knows!" said her mother. "All I know is that your father and your 'best friend' are quite a team. He's full of a lot of bad advice, and she's full of a lot of bad ideas about how to carry out his bad advice. And you! You stay away from Iris! She's a loser."

Maggie stared at her mother. "Can I tell you something?" she asked in an unsteady voice. "If you want to talk about losers, talk about Mr Newton. And his loser Badge Butt liar nephew. But don't talk about Iris."

Maggie stepped a little closer to her mother. "You think I'm sorry Mrs Hall slapped Mr Newton's face? I could never be sorry Mrs Hall slapped Mr Newton's face. He hates me, Mum. Don't you know that?"

"Oh, come on."

"Mum! It's true. Corky Newton told the kids. His uncle hates me!"

Maggie's mother picked up a rag, flipped it out, and folded it on the workbench. "Relax. Nobody hates you. You just got involved in a scheme. Nobody hates you.''

"Why didn't you stand up for me?" said Maggie. "Why?"

"You need to go to your room to calm down," said her mother.

"Don't you care that somebody hates somebody in your family? Doesn't it make you feel bad?"

"Now," said Maggie's mother, pointig to the door.

Maggie stormed into the house and went to her room without saying hello to Dinah's baby-sitter, who was reading a magazine at the kitchen table.

She flopped onto her bed and turned her face to the wall. She stared at the picture of her grandfather that was hanging beside her bed – her mother's father, wearing dungarees. Wearing dungarees and kneeling by two Irish setters in a field of yellow squash.

Maggie picked at the plaster on the frame.

From the next room she heard sounds like a motorboat might make, heading off somewhere far away.

It was Dinah, snoring.

Why did her mother tell Mr Newton that it was her father's fault she'd got in to trouble all week long? All her father said was that Corky Newton needed a taste of his own medicine.

How long was he going to get blamed for one thing?

She rolled onto her back and stared at the ceiling. How long?

She heard her mother come into the house and talk to the baby-sitter.

She heard the jingling of change and then the front door open and close.

So what if Maggie had called her father's office

instead of calling home? So what if she wanted to talk to Samantha! What was the matter with Samantha?

Maggie heard her mother fill the tea kettle in the kitchen and rattle teacups in the cupboard, then move a chair across the kitchen floor.

Soon the kettle began to whistle softly. Maggie heard her mother pour water into the teacup. And she heard the sounds the spoon made clinking against the cup.

Suddenly Maggie stood up. She opened her underwear drawer and found the black fingerless gloves and put them on.

She walked into the kitchen. "Mum?"

Her mother looked up.

"I hid these," said Maggie, holding up her arms.

Her mother looked down at her tea and blew on it, then took a sip.

"I also hid Dad's Harvard shorts. And Mum? I was wondering if you would take the picture of your father out of my room."

Maggie's mother shoved the table forward and stood up, rattling her teacup and spilling tea into the saucer.

"And I don't want the maple sugar candy that your father sent me," said Maggie. "Tell him not to send me maple sugar candy from Vermont. I hate candy shaped like leaves."

"Maggie, you love maple sugar candy shaped like leaves."

"No, I don't!" shouted Maggie.

She looked at the wall. "Not any more, I don't."

Her mother walked over to where Maggie was standing. "You don't want a picture of your grandfather?"

"No."

Maggie looked down at her hands. "My God," said her mother. "You're trembling."

She knelt down and tried to take Maggie's hands, but Maggie pulled them away. She leaned back against the kitchen wall and closed her eyes. Tears rolled past her ears and down her neck. "Tell me why you put a picture of my father in a box marked 'dump,' " she whispered.

Her mother didn't answer.

"Tell me!" cried Maggie.

"Maggie, please," said her mother in a gentle voice. "Won't you look at me?"

But Maggie turned her head away. "Tell me why you hate my dad."

"Why I hate your father? How could I hate your father, when he gave me you – and Dinah?"

Maggie shrugged.

"I'm trying to tell you something. Maggie! Look at me, please," said Maggie's mother, and her eyes filled with tears. "I still love your father. It's been two years, but God! It's hard not to be married to him – even when I don't want to be married to him any more. And it's hard to imagine him in another woman's arms." She closed her eyes. "I've been confused," she whispered. "It's hard to let go of the past, hard to know what to keep and what to throw away. I'm sorry I threw away the picture of your father. I'm sorry. I was wrong."

She paused. "So many things have changed! I've wanted to hold on to you." She took Maggie's hands and held them against her cheek. "You're my baby, Maggie. I remember when you took your first breath of air! Now you're growing up. But I really don't know

130

how to let you grow up. And I don't know how to share you with your father. Or Samantha. Or Iris!"

She stood up and pulled Maggie close to her. "But I know I want to learn."

Maggie wrapped her arms round her mother and they stood there, hugging each other and saying nothing – just rocking back and forth and holding on.

# 16

"How do I look?" said Maggie. She held out the cuffs of the Harvard shorts with her hands and bowed.

Her mother was on her hands and knees, rummaging around under the workbench.

She looked at Maggie. "How did you make your fringe stick straight up?"

"Egg whites," said Maggie. "What do you think?"

"I think you look fabulous. And I think if you sat in the plant stand you could pass for a cactus."

Maggie smiled a little.

Her mother smiled back. "Did Mrs Fuller say okay about the band?"

"Yes," said Maggie. "She said 'anything to get rid of Iris.'"

"Did she say Iris could go out to get a pizza with us?"

"Yes. She said the longer we keep her over here, the better."

Her mother crawled farther under the workbench. "Well, I'll be darned," she said. She pulled out a wooden box. "Look at these." She picked up a small glass bottle and read the label out loud: "Duncan E-Z Stroke liquid underglaze, Dusty Rose." She unscrewed the lid. "See?" she said to Maggie. "Still okay, after all these years."

She stood up and whacked the dust from her knees.

Then, with a grunt, she picked up the box of underglazes and set them on the workbench. "Where's Dinah?"

"She'll be out in a minute," said Maggie. "Iris and I are letting her be our first audience. She says she has to change into something fancier." She sighed. "Perkins is going to be her date. She claims he's wearing a tuxedo."

Maggie's mother plugged in the ceramic lamp with elephants on it. "Thank you for pulling this out of the rubbish," she said. "It's come in handy out here." She held it in the air so she could see what was at the back of the cabinet above her head and pulled down an enormous green book. "And it's made me think. Maybe I should turn this garage into a work space for my pottery."

She turned to Maggie. "What do you think?"

"I think if you turned the plant stand upside down and put it on your head, you'd look like the Statue of Liberty," said Maggie.

They looked at each other for a moment.

"And yes, it's a good idea," said Maggie.

Her mother put down the lamp. "I could buy a little electric kiln. I could pin up some plastic all around here," she said, running her hand along the edge of the workbench, "and make a place to keep the clay damp. Is that a good idea?"

"A very good idea," said Maggie.

Her mother handed her the book. "This belongs with the rest of Dad's things."

Maggie walked over to a cardboard box that had DUMP crossed out and DAVE written above it. She put the book in the box. The she pulled out the sweatshirt with the cracked rubber dove on the front and held it up against her chest.

"Don't get your eye on that," her mother told her. "Fold it right back up, just the way it was." She looked at Maggie. "It's a message from me – to your dad."

Maggie carefully put the sweatshirt back into the box, closed the flaps and sat on it.

"You know," she said, "I've been wondering –"

"What have you been wondering, Maggie?"

"I've been wondering – how come Corky Newton got away with everything?"

"Everything?" said Maggie's mother. "I wouldn't say he got away with everything."

"He got away with wrecking my lunch."

"Yes, he did get away with that."

"And lying."

"And lying – yes," said her mother. "But he didn't get away with everything." She paused. "Because in the end he has to be Corky Newton.

"But you, Maggie," she said, "you can be you."

Maggie thought a moment. "And also," she told her mother, "also in the end I bet he gets nailed by Iris."

Her mother said nothing.

"Bet you he does," said Maggie. She clopped over and stood in front of the mirror with one hand on her hip. She tucked in, then untucked, her shirt, watching her reflection in the glass. She unsnapped her sleeves and rolled them up, and put up her collar.

"Remember," said her mother. "Tell Iris I said you could *wear* those alligator pumps, not *paint* them."

"Right," said Maggie. She moved closer to the mirror and tipped her head and stared at her nose. Then she opened her mouth and slid her tongue across the front teeth, examining the one that was growing in crooked.

It looked okay.

Maggie turned sideways. She pulled on the front of her shirttails and took a long look at the cowboys galloping across her chest. Then she peered into her shirt.

Everything seemed the same.

She pulled her fingerless gloves up tighter, up to her elbows. And she carefully moved the bow in her hair to one side. "Love you, Mum," she said. She made the bow a little wider.

"Me too," said her mother.

*Carolyn Bear*

## UNDER DIFFERENT STARS

"*Zig:* I was really enjoying myself now. I thought with satisfaction how in the morning I would tell Bragge that I'd got all the way home with the ice-maiden.

*Julia:* I couldn't believe it. There he was wiping his filthy sneakers on our doormat. Settling down in the one other armchair. My father was giving him a beer . . ."

It's just too incredible, Julia thought. This guy'd got some nerve. He follows me, scrounges his bus-fare off me, and somehow manages to get himself invited for dinner. Who the hell does he think he is?

*Tony Drake*

## NO TIME TO SAY GOODBYE


Martin was bowled over by Cath. Imagine an attractive, smart, well-heeled girl like her being interested in him. And everything was so easy with her – Cath led and Martin just followed. He liked her a lot, even though he didn't always approve of the things she got up to.

Martin didn't even mind about Cath's friend Gee, who always seemed to be around. He had heard rumours about the sort of businesses Gee was mixed up in, but he was fun, he knew how to have a good time. One thing was for sure, Martin's life was more exciting for knowing Cath and Gee. The trouble was, he didn't know what their game was – until he was in it up to his neck . . .

*Betsy Haynes*

## THE GREAT BOYFRIEND TRAP

Scotti Wheeler and Lorna Markham are not only neighbours, they're best friends too, so they tell each other *everything* . . . well, almost! Lorna is stunned when she finds out that Scotti has a crush on her brother Skip – and then Scotti discovers that Lorna has a crush on Fletcher Holloway – who Scotti thinks is a nerd!

But once the two friends get over their double shock, they have to find a way to get Skip and Fletcher to notice them – so *The Great Boyfriend Trap* is planned . . .

Jean Richardson

## MUSICAL CHAIRS

Four young musicians enter a music competition ...

Philip, a talented cellist, needs to compensate for his father's failure to make the grade as a musician.

Vicky has the advantage of inherited talent and influential parents, but resents the obligation to follow in their footsteps.

Tod, looking for the quickest way to the top, finds there is more to playing the violin than a brilliant technique.

Jane, the only one not at a specialist music school, desperately needs a better teacher.

For Philip, Vicky, Tod and Jane, the competition is not just a matter of winning, it's a time of facing up to the world and learning about themselves.

*"excellent atmosphere and tension."*
The Birmingham Post

*"there is a sturdy honesty about this plain direct interweaving of four destinies."*
Growing Point

*"amazing in the way it conveys the pleasures of playing and listening to music. It is impossible for me to say how much I enjoyed this book."*
Lancashire Book Award Reviewer

# A Selected List of Fiction from Mammoth

While every effort is made to keep prices low, it is sometimes necessary to increase prices at short notice. Mammoth Books reserves the right to show new retail prices on covers which may differ from those previously advertised in the text or elsewhere.

The prices shown below were correct at the time of going to press.

| | | | | |
|---|---|---|---|---|
| ☐ | 416 13972 8 | **Why the Whales Came** | Michael Morpurgo | £2.50 |
| ☐ | 7497 0034 3 | **My Friend Walter** | Michael Morpurgo | £2.50 |
| ☐ | 7497 0035 1 | **The Animals of Farthing Wood** | Colin Dann | £2.99 |
| ☐ | 7497 0136 6 | **I Am David** | Anne Holm | £2.50 |
| ☐ | 7497 0139 0 | **Snow Spider** | Jenny Nimmo | £2.50 |
| ☐ | 7497 0140 4 | **Emlyn's Moon** | Jenny Nimmo | £2.25 |
| ☐ | 7497 0344 X | **The Haunting** | Margaret Mahy | £2.25 |
| ☐ | 416 96850 3 | **Catalogue of the Universe** | Margaret Mahy | £1.95 |
| ☐ | 7497 0051 3 | **My Friend Flicka** | Mary O'Hara | £2.99 |
| ☐ | 7497 0079 3 | **Thunderhead** | Mary O'Hara | £2.99 |
| ☐ | 7497 0219 2 | **Green Grass of Wyoming** | Mary O'Hara | £2.99 |
| ☐ | 416 13722 9 | **Rival Games** | Michael Hardcastle | £1.99 |
| ☐ | 416 13212 X | **Mascot** | Michael Hardcastle | £1.99 |
| ☐ | 7497 0126 9 | **Half a Team** | Michael Hardcastle | £1.99 |
| ☐ | 416 08812 0 | **The Whipping Boy** | Sid Fleischman | £1.99 |
| ☐ | 7497 0033 5 | **The Lives of Christopher Chant** | Diana Wynne-Jones | £2.50 |
| ☐ | 7497 0164 1 | **A Visit to Folly Castle** | Nina Beachcroft | £2.25 |

All these books are available at your bookshop or newsagent, or can be ordered direct from the publisher. Just tick the titles you want and fill in the form below.

**Mandarin Paperbacks**, Cash Sales Department, PO Box 11, Falmouth, Cornwall TR10 9EN.

Please send cheque or postal order, no currency, for purchase price quoted and allow the following for postage and packing:

UK          80p for the first book, 20p for each additional book ordered to a maximum charge of £2.00.

BFPO       80p for the first book, 20p for each additional book.

Overseas    £1.50 for the first book, £1.00 for the second and 30p for each additional book
including Eire   thereafter.

NAME (Block letters) ................................................................................................................................

ADDRESS ..................................................................................................................................................

....................................................................................................................................................................

....................................................................................................................................................................